THE DREAMS

OF

KIM KWANG-CHUL

John Eenigenburg

FIRST EDITION, JUNE 2013

ISBN 978-0-9858251-0-2

Cover art by Peter Nagy

Printed in the United States of America
Third Printing

THE DREAMS

OF

KIM KWANG-CHUL

She slept soundly, unaware of his presence. Even if she had not slept so soundly, he knew that he could look upon her with impunity. She would not have the slightest suspicion that he was there. He resisted the temptation to disturb her in any way, to touch her for instance. He was content just to watch her, to suck in her beauty with his eyes.

She slept on a yo with an ibul drawn over her. He wondered whether she was naked. He could easily confirm this by lifting up the ibul. But he wanted to preserve the sense of anticipation he felt and so he did nothing.

A lamp standing on the ondol floor remained dimly lit, casting a subdued glow into the furthest corners of the room. Was she afraid of the dark? This was not an unreasonable fear.

He approached her yo. She lay with her face half-buried in her pillow. Her hair cascaded across her cheek. The sound of her breathing was deep and regular. There was no reason to believe she was feigning sleep.

"Are you asleep?" he asked softly, just to be sure. "Or are you just pretending to be asleep?" There was no response.

He rested on his haunches. She was sleeping on her right side with one hand, her left, half-clenched in front of her face and on her pillow. Her lips were slightly parted and her thumb was so close to her mouth that she might have been sucking on it at one time. The thumb, however, was dry.

She was still. She might have been dead for all appearances. He knew she was not dead. His senses told him that she was alive and vulnerable. Reaching out and

1

being careful not to touch her, he placed his hand near her mouth. He felt her breath gently wash over his fingers; the sensation thrilled him. He sat quietly watching her in the suffused light, continually sucking in her beauty with his eyes.

What would she do if she knew that he was there, next to her, at that very moment? Undoubtedly she would scream. Instinctively he tensed and waited for her eyes to open. They did not.

He studied her face. Her face was half-obscured by strands of long black hair. Her eyes were hidden beneath her hair. Her left cheek was turned up, resembling a white lotus. Her chin was smoothly chiseled. Her pale neck disappeared beneath the ibul.

He thought that she was remarkably beautiful. Her beauty was particularly enhanced by her youth. He judged her to be about twenty-two or twenty-three years old, a few years younger than he. He told himself that in another few years her beauty would reach its apex and begin to wane. She was a flower whose time would soon come to pass.

He studied her lips. Her lips were dark, full, and fresh like ripe figs. He felt that many males and perhaps even females had tried to kiss her. He wondered whether she had succumbed to them. There was something strong and defiant about her that he could sense even as she slept. He wondered whether she was a virgin.

The scent of her body wafted up. It was a clean scent. He sniffed her hair. The fragrant aroma of red ginseng shampoo filled his nostrils. Her whole body was suffused with an air of cleanliness. This only confirmed in his mind her purity and innocence. The cleanliness of her body, he thought, reflected the condition of her soul.

She stirred on the yo. He watched quietly as the fingers of her left hand gently massaged the tip of her nose, then slid up to a corner of her eye and rubbed there. Her mouth opened wide to issue a yawn. He could see her perfectly straight white teeth glistening through the strands of black hair that fell across her face. Her gums appeared fresh and pink like raw salmon. She closed her mouth. The tip of her tongue appeared and moistened her lips – an act of sublime delicacy.

Looking down upon her, he saw that there was an expression of sadness on her face. Something had troubled her. Indeed, something had touched her so intensely that in doing so it had left its shadow upon her – an indelible mark that even sleep could not efface. Nor could the tenderness of her features hide her sadness. And yet this sadness did not blemish, but only enhanced, her natural beauty.

And what was that which glimmered upon her cheeks? The stain of tears, recently dried, was apparent. She had been crying. Had she done so while she had been awake? It was impossible to tell. Conceivably, she had cried herself to sleep. He wondered what might be the source of her anguish. What could move one so budding with life to such evident despondency? For the briefest moment her sadness stirred within him a similar sentiment. But the moment passed as swiftly as it had arisen, and the familiar emptiness that usually pervaded him replaced the feeling of lugubriousness.

He saw that her beauty was not flawless. There was a small, almost imperceptible scar just below the outer corner of her left eye. He took the little finger of his right hand and softly stroked her lashes. She responded to his touch and her eyelids fluttered like the wings of a butterfly.

3

Should he lift her eyelids, force them open? What lurked behind them? What dreams and memories could be found there? What life pulsated behind her closed eyelids? He pressed his fingers gently down upon them, trying to feel in the palpitating movements of her eyes the secrets they held. For a brief moment he was sensible of something akin to a memory. Was it his memory or hers? He tried to seize the images that flew through his mind, but he could not do so. They were too elusive, too fleeting, to capture. Yet he sensed that in those evanescent reflections something of her could be known.

Had the images been born of her desires? Were these wings of thought the stirrings of her own unconscious longings, the subtle manifestations of her latent yearnings? He abruptly felt that she wanted to die.

"Why should you want to die?" he muttered, pulling his fingers from her eyes. "Someone as beautiful as you has everything to live for."

Rising, he stepped over to the window. A full moon hung over Seoul like a bloated circle. The bright glow of the city lights soaked the night sky. The window was closed; the room was air-conditioned. Perhaps she slept soundly because of the chill of the room. Her room was as cold as a mausoleum. And she was like a corpse lain out on a slab. Only her shallow breathing betrayed the truth. Would her lips be cool? Certainly there was an iciness to her porcelain beauty.

Standing by the window, he suddenly felt confined by the four walls of the room. The walls seemed to move in, redefining the interior space. A powerful craving welled up in him. He whipped around and stared fiercely at the figure on the yo.

What made her so special? Why should he linger above her without surrendering to his natural appetency? What kind of girl might she be to hold him in abeyance for so long?

Yet while he could force himself upon her at any moment, there was poignancy in delay. Now she was at the height of her allurement. Now her sadness was amplified a hundredfold. Now, poised between two extremes, callow innocence and utter despoliation, she was brimming with vitality.

Perhaps her sadness was rooted in an intuitive apprehension of her fate. Certainly she must have sensed his presence in the room even as she slept. A subtle change had come over her, an alteration in the unseen energy that flowed from her being. Though she did not stir, he knew that somehow she had become aware of him. He was sure that she was dreaming of him.

He moved from the window. In a corner of the room stood a bookcase. Among the many volumes he saw were the ancient classics, the *Samguk sagi* and the *Samguk yusa.* These were books he himself owned – a coincidence?

He took a leather-bound volume off one of the shelves and saw that a bookmark was stuck between its pages. Opening the book, one of the songs of Ch'ŏyong met his eye. He was familiar with the story: while in the service of King Hŏngang of Silla, Ch'ŏyong returned home late one night to find his wife in bed with a demon. He read:

> *I reveled all night*
> *Under the capital's moonlight;*
> *Home I then sped*
> *And beheld four legs in my bed!*
> *Two legs I knew,*

Two legs were new;
Below lay my love,
But what creature lay above?

Had she a premonition of his coming? He decided it was just a fluke. Closing the book, he replaced it on the shelf and whirled around and peered at the sleeping figure.

Cautiously approaching the yo, he reached for her ibul and carefully drew it back. Her breasts revealed themselves in the moonlight like shimmering pearls on a sandy white beach. He pulled the ibul completely from her and let it drop on the floor.

Poised above her, he lay his hand upon her flat, smooth belly and felt the delicious warmth of her skin and the surprising tautness of her muscles. Her small, firm breasts jutted out haughtily, a sure sign of her proud nature. Her rosy nipples stood in stark contrast to her pallid skin. As he reached out to touch one of her breasts, he hesitated.

The moment he did so, her eyes abruptly opened and he was staring directly into them.

Kwang-Chul abruptly woke up. He immediately rued having had the misfortune to do so, for his dream of the girl was fresh upon his mind.

Rolling over on his bed, he buried his head in his pillow and closed his eyes. He wanted to return to the dream, to shut out the bright morning sunshine and descend into the realm of darkness where his memory of the girl dwelled.

For several minutes he lay, sweetly recalling the delicious sensations of his dream. He wished that he could lie there forever, savoring his memory over and over. He wondered:

Is she the One?

Kwang-Chul believed that there existed in the world one girl meant for him and him alone. She would be a girl unlike any he had ever known. The love he would feel for this girl would be no ordinary love. All other loves, all other passions, would seem lifeless by comparison. And just as his love for her would not be ordinary, she herself would be no ordinary girl. She would be a girl of unsurpassed purity and beauty. In his mind, sexual purity and beauty were natural correlatives.

Years before he had dreamt about such a girl while he slept and, for a time, she came to him quite often in his dreams. She had a mark of great beauty: a birth mote in her eye in the shape of a yin taiji. He had longed for the day when she would appear to him not as a dream, but as someone marvelously alive and real. Without knowing why, he had believed that one day she would appear to him out of nowhere, just like that.

The last time he had dreamt of her, they were standing on the slope of a pine-covered mountain. In the misty sunlight filtering through the trees her beauty seemed to him as if it belonged to the heavens and not the earth. The sadness in her eyes was haunting.

When he woke up from his dream, he had a foreboding that he would not see her again. He was correct. After that, he did not dream of her anymore. He tried many times to bring her into his dreams at night, but without success.

For a long time after that he had wondered whether she really existed, and if she did, whether she had tried to dream of him as he had tried to dream of her. When all of his efforts went for naught, he decided that she really didn't exist after all. He gave up trying and over time his love for her faded. He had comforted himself with the belief that: *Love is an illusion, just like everything else in this world.*

The room was hot and stuffy. Kwang-Chul threw back his wrinkled sheet, exposing his naked body. His skin was dazzling white in the morning sunlight. His muscles were soft and ill-defined; he was overweight and out-of-shape. A layer of sweat covered his flabby body.

Among his friends, Kwang-Chul was considered something of a loner. He never completely enjoyed the company of his male companions. Their conversations, amounting to inarticulate gab and crude jokes, made him feel uneasy. Whereas most of the fellows he knew enjoyed chatting about girls, and particularly their successes with them, he did not. He felt guided by high principles. He disdained the typically vulgar conversations of his friends and their endless boasting. He also disliked the way they talked about money all the time, about how easy it was to seduce a girl when one had a little cash in the pocket – as if money was the answer to everything.

"Of course it is," Chan-Woo, his childhood friend, once told him. Chan-Woo was a rough sort of fellow who had few scruples where girls were concerned. His conquests were legendary among those who knew him. Everyone heard it said of him that he never did it with a girl without first killing a turtle and drinking its blood for power – just like men did in the ancient days. This story was enough to cement his reputation.

"All women are whores," Chan-Woo had said. "All they want is money and they're willing to do anything to get it. Anything! And the ones who tell you they're not interested in money are lying. Don't let them fool you. One way or another, they'll be sure to put the squeeze on a guy!"

Kwang-Chul was reluctant to believe this. "Surely not all women!"

"*All* women, Kwang-Chul!" exclaimed Chan-Woo emphatically. "That's why they're women! They'll spread their legs for any guy who'll take them out and feed them a meal and drop some cash on them. Of course they'll convince themselves they're doing it for love. Love!" Spittle flew in all directions from Chan-Woo's thick lips. "Women don't know the first thing about love! They're too self-serving. Frankly, there's not a sincere one among the lot."

Kwang-Chul despised this talk all the more because deep down he knew that there was more than a grain of truth to what Chan-Woo had said. Seoul was fraught with young women whose painted lips and intimate caresses could be purchased for the price of a good meal and a night out at one of the latest clubs. Yet these girls were so beautiful that it appeared to him that they belonged to another world altogether, a world of long ago, a world unstained by the vices of modern society.

Besides, with the opposite sex he felt terribly awkward. Not at all good-looking, he was self-conscious and found it impossible to talk to the girls he knew. He was always afraid they would laugh at him or else mark him as a sensitive poet or just too effeminate in his nature.

Kwang-Chul hated the world because it was corrupt and full of injustice and pettiness. He wanted to keep himself undefiled. He saw the stains of defilement as black clouds darkening the blue skies of his true nature; so, too, was the world darkened because the light of man's nature was everywhere obscured. The conviction that if he should keep himself pure, he would somehow attain a happiness that others could not sat aglow like a blazing fire in the nucleus of his being.

Some days, when he was feeling especially depressed, he believed that the happiness he sought was attainable only in death.

Secretly he saw himself as better than others and more deserving. He was not at all like those he knew. His heart was not in business or in making money. He did not know precisely what he was suited for, if anything at all, but there was still time enough to ascertain the winds of his fate. He was only twenty-five and had yet to make his mark upon the world. For the time being, and out of a sense of uncertainty about his future, he would content himself with his situation.

Kwang-Chul felt that, by some inscrutable act of fate, he alone was blessed with a noble and magnanimous nature that others did not have. It was a marvelous sign that he had a black mole on his skull. Kangsu had had such a mole, and all had said that this was a sign of his extraordinariness. Also, Kwang-Chul was a virgin and he took special pride in this fact. He had never even kissed a girl. Yet, in spite of this, there were times when he hated his own innocence and exalted sense of virtue. His friends drank, smoked, chased girls, and, in general, behaved as if nothing in the world mattered except the pursuit of their own pleasures. He had nothing but contempt for them, but he longed to be one of them.

The thought of his own ordinariness tormented him increasingly – the suspicion that he was not as remarkable as he believed himself to be, that he was no different and no better than all the rest. If he could not be superior to others, morally or otherwise, there could be no prospect of joy in his life. Feeling apart from others provided him with his only opportunity for happiness. Yet with this feeling of separateness came an intense loneliness that was often unbearable.

These antipodes, his belief in his extraordinariness and the nagging suspicion that he was just like everyone else, dwelled inside of him like two armies poised and ready for war. Sometimes he felt as though the only resolution to this inner turmoil was to have been born in another era, in a time and place where a man was judged not so much by how he appeared, but by what he did.

In his reveries, he imagined himself as he might have lived had he been born centuries ago. He saw himself as a wise sage or monk in ancient Paekche, the noblest and most spiritual kingdom ever to grace the earth – or so he believed. His eyes misted with longing for those times gone by. No modern ruler would ever issue a decree prohibiting the killing of all living things, yet this happened in Paekche just a few years after the monk Hyech'ong traveled to Japan and taught the Vinaya rules of discipline, which was not so many years after King Sŏng ordered the Sanskrit texts of Wu-fen lü to be brought from India for translation. How could he not find happiness in a land of such lofty aspirations? Where royal decree had even ordered that all domestic birds be set free and all hunting and fishing tools burned? Certainly he had been born in the wrong time!

Tears gushed in his eyes whenever he read from the *Samguk yusa* and the *Samguk sagi* the stories of those pure spirits who flourished so long ago. Each time he thought about it, he cursed in his heart war-mongering Silla, which had allied itself with T'ang China to trample this wonderful flower of civilization. Silla blood flowed through his veins and this made his pain even more bitter and distressing.

His heart cried out for a return to those simpler times, for a time when men's motives were clear and it was possible to discern where one stood in relation to things. There would be no blurred lines between right and wrong, between heroes and villains. Things would be profoundly apparent: evil would be indisputably so, manifest, and deserving of retribution. But, as things stood, he was frustrated by his inability to perceive a clear antagonist. The modern world was too turbid, too dark and shadowy. It was not always possible to distinguish right from wrong, good from bad, the just from the unjust.

He knew that the lines had been blurred within him. He enjoyed going to the movies and he bought all the latest music. He dressed fashionably to soothe a modest streak of vanity. His high ideals at times gave way to an embarrassing delight in ordinary pleasures. He was especially fond of Glade, the drinking house his mother owned in the It'aewon-dong district of Seoul, where he waited on tables and watched the beautiful hostesses while they sipped on their soju and ate their anju. But he never allowed himself to flirt with any of them. Though he longed to chat with them on familiar terms, it was more satisfying to pretend that he didn't care, that he was above that sort of thing. He preferred just to keep to himself and admire their beauty, while in the back of his mind always lurked the thought:

12

I'd give anything, just anything, to spend the night with a girl like this.

He cursed himself on those occasions. Just once, why couldn't he let his guard down and muster the courage to talk to one of the hostesses who worked at Glade? Time and time again, he envisioned himself in the embrace of a lovely girl whose only concern was to satisfy his desires. The sweetness of the encounter would remain within him long after she had left, spreading through him like a slow poison, numbing his sensibilities. With the passage of time, the memory of the indiscretion would become diluted. But would it be effaced completely? In any event, his fear always got the better of him and held him in check. Not tonight, not tonight . . .

He knew that if he succumbed to just any girl, he would never be the same. If he were indeed different and better than everyone else, he would be so no longer.

But what had his discipline achieved? For all his marvelous self-control, he was intensely unhappy and dissatisfied with himself. His natural desire, which he had suppressed for so long, lay like a sleeping, coiled serpent in the pit of his loins, waiting to be freed. He feared the day this serpent would be unleashed. He feared its dark, destructive power; it was more powerful than he and all his principles put together. He was afraid this serpent would one day destroy him and all that he believed in.

There was a knock on his bedroom door. He grabbed his rumpled sheet and concealed his nakedness.

"Come in."

The door quietly opened and a slender, lithe woman entered the room. His mother was forty-five years old with large, clear eyes set in a cream-white oval face. Her long black hair was pinned into a neat bun. She exuded a natural, healthy beauty. Kim Kyung-A was a widow; Kwang-Chul's father had passed away years before. His mother had never remarried although there had been several prospects.

"It's time for you to get up," she said, walking over to the window and opening it wide. They occupied a small suite of rooms directly over Glade. "It's so hot in here. How can you stand it?"

He sat up and rubbed his eyes. Surrounded by sunlight, his mother floated in a sea of macula. "Good morning. What time is it?"

"Almost seven," she said, flourishing a smile. Her teeth shone like freshwater pearls. "I'm going to start breakfast now."

He watched his mother glide effortlessly across the room. She left the room as unobtrusively as she had entered and silently closed the door behind her.

As an adolescent he used to think of his mother as the most beautiful woman he had ever seen – her beauty was a source of particular torment for him. His mother's extraordinary beauty and the impossible happiness he sought were of the same glittering, untouchable substance.

For a time, he had fallen in love with her and, because of this, he had hated his father. He became incensed whenever he considered how his mother's fabulous beauty had been diminished by the ordinariness of his father. His father's ordinariness had been an ugly pall that obscured the beauty of everything it touched. In his mind, being ordinary was a sin or worse. Ordinariness could neither beget nor compliment anything beautiful; it could only detract from beauty's light. How could his mother ever have married such an unexceptional man?

But it especially had tortured him to know that each night his father actually possessed his mother's beauty – that

14

incredible beauty which infused his head with dangerous thoughts. In bed each night, he had felt that the sweetness of the purity he strived for in his adolescent heart was nothing compared with the savoriness of the terrible longing he felt in the burrows of his flesh. He agonized over the knowledge that only a thin wall separated him from this marvelous, incomprehensible beauty that he yearned for madly but which could never be his. In his anguish he determined that it was necessary for him to more completely see his mother's beauty.

He did. It happened solely by chance one sweltering midsummer, when he was thirteen . . .

He had been playing outdoors on a hot, humid afternoon. He had returned home, maybe it was just before noon, to get something cool and refreshing to drink. The door to the apartment was unlocked, as it sometimes was. He had walked in without ado, dripping of sweat. Almost immediately, he heard deep, melodious, plaintive sounds. His mother was sitting alone at her kayageum, eyes closed, dreamily fingering its strings. Except for the movement of her fingers, she looked as if she were asleep. She was naked. Her hair was damp and hung in thick black tangles down her pale neck. Softly, as if treading on unbearably thin ice, he edged closer. Her breasts, full and almost bursting with womanhood, submitted themselves for inspection. They were a fantastic sight to behold, glistening globes of dream-like reality that made his eyelids flutter with disbelief. His eyes sank down to the black tousled fabric between her legs, and suddenly he sensed his own burgeoning manhood, its raw power emanating from somewhere deep in his youthful flesh, and he trembled with joy.

She was not aware of his presence. He moved breathlessly closer, inexorably drawn to the mystery of his mother's flesh that had haunted his imagination for so many nights. How he had yearned to see her like this! And now she was there, tantalizingly close, so exhilaratingly close, but oh, so impossible to touch. His eyes sucked in the marvelous sight of her nakedness, while his tender hands clenched themselves into fists of frustration.

Abruptly she came out of her reverie. Through her long lashes she saw him standing there, observing her in deliberate silence. Her delicate hand froze in the air above the kayageum. Nothing was said, not a movement was made. He felt as if the passage of time had magically ceased.

Their eyes met. His were filled with embarrassment, hers were accusatorial. He was suddenly sensible of her lips trembling with fierce anger, while her eyes flashed furiously, *How could you?* The hot fervor which had possessed him only a moment ago was replaced by a cold, terrible fear and an overwhelming sense of shame. *I'm sorry.* He wanted to beg her forgiveness, but the words stuck in his throat like lumps of stone. When at last she folded her hands over her breasts and legs, like a butterfly gently folding its wings, he bolted from the room.

For the next several hours, he remained secluded in his bedroom, suffering with shame. But, as the day wore on, the consciousness of his impropriety faded and was instead supplanted by the absolute knowledge, more real than any other, that finally he had glimpsed his mother naked, as he had long desired to do. Ecstatically, he thought, *Today I saw my mother's boji. I can't believe what a fantastic day this has been!* He savored the realization that his mother would always carry within her, like an unwanted child, the embarrassing awareness that he had seen her and had possessed her beauty – that somehow, by having glimpsed the smooth loveliness of her impeccable skin, and the forbidden area between her legs, he had made her beauty his own, if only for a moment. For the rest of the afternoon, visions of her sitting at her kayageum, her splendid flesh bewitching his soul, simmered in his brain. Secretly he hoped that she would call him into her room on some pretext or another. After all, he should be chastised; he deserved as much. *Come to me, Kwang-Chul, you bad little boy. Mom's got to teach you a lesson.* But she did not call him, and, by evening, he had irreversibly linked the sweet beauty of her flesh to the unattainable happiness he sought. By that time, he was burning with fever.

Rising from bed, Kwang-Chul sat down on floor cushions in front of a low desk without attempting to conceal his nakedness. From atop his desk, he picked up a thick notebook with the words *Dream Journal* crudely printed in black ink, by his own hand, on the cover. He opened this notebook to the first clean page. Selecting a black and gold fountain pen, he began recording his dream of the night before.

He wrote swiftly, choosing his words without measuring their weight or quality, and omitting unnecessary description. He merely wanted to capture the highlights of his dream. Later, when he went back to the journal and perused what he had written, he would be able to sufficiently recall the details of his dream.

Besides, he wasn't too good at putting his thoughts into words; there was considerable difference between his reminiscences of the night and how they came out on paper. For instance, when he remembered how the girl's beauty had seemed to him like rays of light that transformed the turbid heaviness of the night into a pellucid loveliness, he couldn't find the words to aptly describe his impressions. He jotted down, *She was beautiful.* And recalling the way he felt when her soft, sensitive lips touched his, as if the impossible happiness which had eluded him for so long had suddenly revealed itself as an attainable ideal, he wrote, *I kissed her and it felt wonderful.*

After he had described to his satisfaction the previous night's dream, he read over the passage to make sure he had not forgotten anything. As he relived the dream in his thoughts, he could feel the girl's presence and the sweet sensations of the night before so strongly that he was almost convinced that it was not just a dream. He mused, as he put the capped tip of the pen into his mouth, "Was my dream merely the rendering of my subconscious and nothing more? Or does this girl really exist?"

Staring blankly at the large stone figurine on his desk, he recalled once again how her bedroom had appeared to him in his dream, seeing against the turbid backdrop of his mind her pale curtains, the pearl-white vanity, and the white bookcase filled with an array of books.

Even though her room appeared to him only in his imagination, it was warm and familiar. Moreover, he felt that the sight of her things connected him to her in some definite way. Why *couldn't* the girl be real? But, as he ruminated upon the irrefutable reality of the desk and journal in front of him, and the implausibility of this notion, seeds of uncertainty were deposited in his mind.

The painted figurine on his desk, a dancer of the Pongsan masked dance, came into focus. Gnawing at the tip of his pen, he wondered, "Does she really own the books I saw?" Knitting his brow, he tried to recall the titles of the books he had seen, but they fluctuated hazily in his mind.

He picked up the journal from his desk and placed it in his lap. Pressing his fingers to his forehead, he soberly reflected upon its contents.

Contained in the journal was a record of his dreams. He hated himself for keeping such a journal. The desires he so fervently repressed during the course of the day unfurled themselves in all their ugliness during the night.

To make matters worse, he could not refrain from keeping the journal. What had begun as an occasional practice grew into a compulsion. He contemned himself whenever he read from the text he had inscribed in permanent ink on its crisp white pages.

January 30. Last night a new hostess came to work at Glade – a wide-mouthed beauty with bright, lively eyes named Hyun-Jung. She arrived just before we opened and we exchanged a few pleasantries. Later, I returned to chat her up while she smoked a cigarette. After Glade closed . . .

"I followed her home," he muttered, eagerly turning the page. At the time, he had felt a vague satisfaction in knowing where she lived. He went home that night and soaked in the bath and conjured up sultry images of her in his mind. Afterwards, when he went to bed, he retraced the path to her apartment building with his thoughts and felt reassured that he would be able to find his way back if he wanted to . . .

He continued to read:

I entered her apartment. It was pitch black inside, but it only took me a minute to find her. She was sound asleep. I slipped into bed with her . . .

After reading a particular passage, the memory of the experience usually left in him a pleasant feeling, not unlike the savory warmth he felt from eating roasted nuts. But once the feeling faded, he was pervaded with shame and self-reproach.

The journal was an abhorrence. If anyone should read it . . .

April 11. Last night I dreamt about the flower girl . . .

For a time he had seen this girl walking past Glade almost every evening. She was always dressed in a fashionable woman's suit, presumably returning home from work each evening. A black purse invariably dangled from a strap on her shoulder. She had thick lips and a clear complexion. Her cheeks were large and her nostrils distended. She was not especially attractive, but still, she had a certain appeal. Her suit shifted fabulously when she walked and from beneath the folds of fabric her womanhood seemed to scream at him, clamoring rudely for his attention. She was about twenty-four years old. He didn't know her name, but ever since the evening he spotted her carrying a bouquet of mugunghwa, he thought of her as the "flower girl." He read:

Her bedroom door was open and I stood in the doorway. She was stretched out in bed with her arms cradled around a pillow. A quilt covered her legs. I climbed into bed with her and took the pillow from her arms. She gave it up without a fuss. I saw that she wore a thin chemise. It clung to her body . . .

He recalled how the flower girl seemed particularly fragile, as if merely touching her might shatter her into pieces . . .

Resting my hand upon her hip, I could feel her sharp bone underneath. My hand slipped under the quilt and touched her flesh. I cupped her knee in my hand and held it momentarily. Then I moved my hand from her knee and let it slowly glide under her chemise . . .

His unfamiliarity with her flesh had sent ripples of excitement through him. Always, the wonderful freshness of a girl who was new and strange to him aroused him considerably.

Thinking back, he remembered how the very next evening the flower girl had paused in front of Glade and peered in. He was wiping one of the tables and happened to glance up just at that moment. They stood face-to-face on opposite sides of the window. Was it just his imagination or had she blushed when she had seen him? In any event, she had averted her gaze and turned away from him. She departed hurriedly, without looking back. It was the last time he had seen her.

Kwang-Chul was repelled by the sight of the journal. Mashing his teeth together, he told himself bitterly, "It should be destroyed."

On several occasions he had taken it into his hands, had been on the verge of shredding its malignant pages, when he had been overcome with doubt and hesitancy.

"How can I rend this into pieces?" This question tormented him each time he felt the weight of the journal in his hands, its potent mass emulating the imponderable heaviness in his heart. "It would be like ripping my own life asunder."

His own being was inexplicably bound up in the immense unreality collected on its pages.

April 25. Last night I dreamt I was walking through the streets of Seodaemun-gu. Suddenly I was overcome by a powerful desire I couldn't control. My flesh ached for a girl . . .

He recalled the madness that had come over him, the raging desire like an unstoppable fire, a steam-like sensation rising from the pores of his flesh, an unappeasable yearning in the hollow of his groin. He had hurtled through the streets of Seodaemun-gu in search of a girl. It didn't matter which girl. Anyone would do . . .

I charged into the nearest building where I came upon a corpulent man sleeping with his young wife. They were both naked. The woman's body glistened in the dark like the underbelly of a fish. Her breasts were huge, with nipples like suckers. I tore at my clothes and pounced upon her like a beast. I pinned her arms down and wrenched her legs apart and rammed my jaji between them. Her eyes flew open. On her face was such a look of horror as I will never forget. She screamed. She didn't stop screaming. No matter, for there was nothing she could do. I was insatiable. I was possessed. I was deranged. I took her like a madman. Her screams became so loud they could have woken up the dead — but not her fat-assed husband. He was snoring merrily . . .

Kwang-Chul pondered the nebulous figures of dream-like reality shimmering like minnows in the convolutions of his brain . . .

I let go of her arms. They thrashed madly about and one of them soundly smacked her fat-assed husband on the nose. He awoke and seeing his wife behaving as if she were in the throes of a fit, began yelling, "Are you alright, dear? What's wrong? Are you having a bad dream?"

Throughout his youth, Kwang-Chul had been plagued by dreams of a sexual nature. In the beginning, he had put them down to the normal aches of adolescence: he supposed the initial flush of sexual awareness had made him susceptible to tantalizingly provocative dreams. There were several girls in middle school for whom he felt pangs of desire whenever he saw the smooth white skin of their arms and legs and their small firm breasts bedeviling him from beneath their school uniforms. How could he describe the rapture which overtook him then, the conflagration which consumed his body and soul in sublime flames of agony and ecstasy? How little his noble aspirations mattered then! With the same supreme delight as when he listened to the plaintive strains of the kayageum or contemplated the serene perfection of the night sky, he absorbed their faultless beauty into his consciousness. Unable to speak with them owing to his shyness, he found a marvelous degree of emancipation in his dreams at night.

The dreams had begun innocently enough. There were dreams of having tea with Hae-Jin in a tiny shop he frequented with his mother; of chatting with Eun-Ju as they walked home from school through a grove of cedar trees that bordered the school grounds; of catching fireflies with

Yoon-Jung in the early evening by the Han river. On these occasions he had behaved with the utmost probity and self-restraint, just as he would have done had he been awake.

But after a time his dreams began to take on sinister characteristics. The innocent meetings with Hae-Jin and the others gave way to dark, sordid visitations in the still of the night. Each time in his dreams he found himself alone with his classmates in their bedrooms while they slept. And his intentions were no longer pure. He simmered with the desire to crawl into bed with them and touch and explore their pristine bodies in ways he could never do while he was awake. But, always, his fear of discovery prevented him from acting upon his desire.

One night everything changed. A dream of Yoon-Jung had taken on a fabulous reality unlike any other and he himself was possessed of an astonishing lucidity. Without any reflection upon the matter, he was confident of the knowledge that everything was not real, including Yoon-Jung. Knowing it was all a dream, the colossal fear which paralyzed him on previous occasions vanished. The usual qualms – What if she woke up? What if her father entered the room? – were marvelously dispelled. Now, unfettered by guilt and fear, and fortified by the certainty that nothing was real, there was absolutely no reason to refrain from becoming physically intimate with the girl who lay insensibly in front of him.

Gazing down at Yoon-Jung, he had felt an overwhelming urgency, as if life itself depended upon the union of their flesh and the fulfillment of his needs. And did it not? For contained within him was another life besides his own: his budding sexuality seemed alien and somehow apart from his own life, yet it had grafted itself onto his unsophisticated sense of being and was now threatening to deprive him of his youthful innocence. Now his adolescent heart was no longer clear and untroubled; dark peril loomed within it. Everything was on the verge of imploding into an ugly chaos. When the fusion of their bodies was complete, all that remained were tangled strands of gossamer reality mixed with a dark, hairy, twisted offal.

At first his dreams presented a disquieting predicament: in them, the purity he so fervidly pursued in his life became a mockery. Once the initial titillation wore off, it was replaced by a singular wrenching discomfort in the center of his abdomen whenever he considered the paucity of his moral character.

For a time he had sought to repress his dreams, but this only brought them on with full vigor. Each night before retiring he read those passages from Wŏn-Hyo's *Palsim suhaeng chang* which exhorted the abandonment of sensual pleasures. For, in some way, was this not the destiny he sought? To completely free himself from his sensual desires? Only then would he be able to discover the true nature of all things which lay behind and beyond the turbid world he lived in. Though he understood with his mind little of the words he read, he knew them with his heart and felt their power and pull on him. Those who were strong and pure in mind and craved not the pleasures of the sensual would be exalted above ordinary men.

He had endeavored, each night as he lay in bed, to dispel all physical sensations by imagining holy scenes, as the Christian saint Ignatius had recommended in his manual for spiritual exercises. However, the rapture that was intended to be produced by concentrating upon such pious eidolons quickly dissolved, the moment he fell asleep, into the very abominations he longed to prevent. How odd, he thought, that his longing for the sublime should have the contrary effect! Was it possible that mystical knowledge of the unseen divine could be cloaked in all kinds of images, including lascivious ones?

He was suddenly sentient of a more mundane type of knowledge: from Glade rose the pungent smell of garlic and onions.

Thinking it over, he realized that as time went by he had pretended not to notice his dreams. It had been easier to ignore them than to suppress them. Of course, he had kept his journal, but, for the most part, he merely accepted his dreams as the fictive renderings of his subconscious and allowed them to run their course. In any event, he had been certain they were harmless.

But now he was not so sure. There was something different about his dream of the girl, something that eluded his immediate comprehension. His mother's approaching footsteps sounded hollow outside his door and he sunk into despondency, trying hard to think what that something might be. Was it the merely the harsh emptiness of his own life juxtaposed against the bountiful sensations of his dreams?

Or was there something mysteriously authentic about his dream? Recalling his dream of Yoon-Jung on that lustrous night so long ago, he remembered how implacably convinced he had been that he indeed was dreaming, and how the quality of his dream had taken on a superb authenticity. But even the marvelous reality of that dream seemed sallow and ersatz when compared with the reality of his dream of the girl. With his heart beating hard, he listened as his mother's footsteps came to a halt outside his door; in the sudden stillness the pounding in his chest seemed strangely amplified. He wondered aloud, "Wouldn't it be something if she were real?"

The prospect was exciting, and he closed his eyes to savor the possibilities.

I could descend in the dead of night and take her any time I want. There would be nothing she could do to protect herself from me. For what would I be to her, but a dream? I wouldn't exist for her except as a figment of her imagination.

The knock on his door and the sound of his mother's voice calling his name snapped him from his thoughts. Closing his journal, he replaced it on his desk and reached for his bed sheet and wrapped it tightly around his waist and mused:

Wouldn't that be something?

Startled, Yoo-Min suddenly woke up. At first glance, she saw a chair with some clothes draped over the top and a pair of nylon stockings lying on the ondol floor. The scene, however, was unfamiliar to her. But as she stared in puzzlement, she slowly recalled that she was at home in bed and that she lived by herself in the Yeouido district of Seoul. Comforted by this realization, she fumbled for the alarm clock beside her yo and saw by its luminous numbers that it was still early in the morning.

What had awoken her? Straining her ear, she listened carefully, but she heard nothing except the peculiar meditative sound of silence – a cold, empty stillness. She searched her mind for a clue. She had been dreaming, that much she was certain, but when she pressed herself further, she could not remember what her dream had been about. She remembered nothing except a numbness that had come over her, a chilling sensation, as if she had fallen asleep in the snow.

She suddenly realized that her skin was tingling with apprehension. Was it because of the dream she was unable to recall or some other reason? Reaching for her ibul she had somehow discarded in her sleep, she drew it up to her neck, appreciating its warmth and feeling just a little protected from uncertain danger.

Dawn was rising when she awoke a second time. Stretching her bare arms above her head, she let out a large yawn; she felt exhausted, like a limp dishrag. The silk curtains in front of the window hung motionless. The window was closed. The room was cool.

Stifling another yawn, she vaguely wondered, *Why am I so tired? Am I coming down with something?* She placed the palm of her hand against her forehead. Her temperature seemed normal.

The apartment she lived in was small but modern. The living room served as her bedroom at night. The kitchen, with a refrigerator and two-burner gas range, adjoined the living area. The bathroom was situated directly opposite the kitchen.

Her yo dominated the floor space. A white vanity with gilded trim and gold-plated handles stood against the left wall. Against the opposite wall was a bookcase with a potted green plant, its leaves drooping languidly, on the top shelf. A flat screen television and chrome stand occupied a corner of the room. On the ondol floor was a portable multimedia player and docking station with loudspeakers. The floor was sparkling clean and polished. Surveying the room through half-closed eyes, Yoo-Min was satisfied. Everything was just the way she liked it.

As she lay on her back listlessly gazing up, a spider in the corner of the ceiling caught her eye. It dangled from a gossamer thread. The spider was black and ugly; it offended her sensibilities. She thought: *Something so ugly has no right to live.* If she had not been squeamish about doing so, she would have squashed it immediately. But then, that would have left a mark on the wall.

Yoo-Min despised ugliness. Ugliness was a weakness, a character flaw. She believed that only beautiful things should exist in the world. In her opinion, she was extraordinarily beautiful. She thought:

If I were ugly, I would know it. But even if I weren't aware of my ugliness, others would be.

What others thought about her mattered a great deal.

She saw herself as a commodity: her considerable beauty increased her worth substantially. But a particular aspect of

29

her sadness was the irrefutable knowledge that her beauty would one day be gone. She feared that any love a man felt for her would last only as long as her looks.

Because of her looks, she never really knew if a man loved her. She only knew when a man wanted her. Every man wanted her.

"They only want me because I'm beautiful," she rued aloud. Her beauty was both the source of her only joy and her considerable melancholy; it placed her in great jeopardy. When her beauty faded, she would be of no use to any man. She would be cast aside like an article of used clothing.

Sometimes she suspected that she didn't really exist, that only her beauty had any reality. So intense and powerful was her beauty that it overshadowed every aspect of her life, almost negating it completely. Yet, in spite of this, she obdurately clung to her beauty for the very life she lacked, drawing upon its strength to sustain her own meager vitality, knowing in her heart that if she could not be beautiful, she had no life at all.

For these reasons, she was not troubled that she could feel little or nothing for others. Empathy was not her strong suit. Rather, she believed it was the extraordinary vigor of her own suffering which constituted the particular source of her genius.

Grabbing her pillow, she crushed it wearily against her chest. She was hungry and thirsty and her head throbbed from too little sleep; gloom engulfed her. She hated waking up to the golden sunshine that invariably streamed through her window shortly after daybreak. Inevitably, a good night's sleep was destroyed in very short order.

Not that her nights were all that serene – most certainly they were not. How many nights had there been where she had tossed and turned while in the throes of some fitful dream? Far too many to count, she thought. Without a doubt, her dreams were usually strange affairs, lending to many restless nights.

At that moment, she recalled a dream she had had during the night. This was a recurring dream that sometimes came to her whenever she felt in touch with a deep, remote, neglected part of herself. Her eyes moistened with sadness as she sensed the terrible loneliness inside her.

The dream had been about her mother. Although her mother had passed away many years before, Yoo-Min still remembered her with unusual clarity. Occasionally she could feel her mother's spirit so strongly that she was convinced her mother was still alive somewhere, in some bright and beautiful heaven, and this comforted her. Yet other times the emptiness within her was so dark and immense that she told herself this was nothing more than wishful thinking. Her mother had died unexpectedly and her sense of loss was still keen.

Staring blankly through her tears at the wall opposite her, she once again saw herself as she had in her dream, as a young girl standing barefoot in the grass at the base of a large hill . . .

Overhead the sun blazed in a lead-blue sky. Shielding her eyes from the sun's stabbing rays, she felt a delicious warmth wrap itself around her like a comfortable garment.

The sweet, ethereal sound of a ch'ojok hauntingly filled the air. At the top of the hill, a splendid-looking woman suddenly appeared. The woman was tall and thin and as pliant as a blade of grass. Yoo-Min thought that she might bend in the slightest breeze. Although the woman's face was obscured by a white veil, Yoo-Min recognized her immediately.

"Mother!"

31

Seized with joy, she began to run full steam up the hill, kicking up her feet like some huge bird madly flapping its wings. She had not gone very far when she suddenly stopped in her tracks. She looked up expectantly; her eyelashes were wet with tears. Her long white legs, thin as bamboo reeds, shook at the knees. Her mother stood above her, shimmering against the earth and sky like an untouchable mirage.

Her heart turned heavy, as if it were weighted with stone. She wanted to run the rest of the way up, but she feared that if she took another step her mother would abruptly disappear. The happiness which infused her heart was placed in uncertain jeopardy.

With a voice soft as dew, her mother called down, "What is wrong, child?"

She clenched her sweat-soaked hands as if to wring an answer from them. What, indeed, was wrong? The question was one of overwhelming import. Everything was wrong, she told herself, everything imaginable under the sun. Heaven and earth were wrong, all of nature was wrong, but most of all, the hurting in her heart was wrong. There was only one conceivable reply:

"I want to be beautiful."

Her breasts ached with this acknowledgment. The whole of her existence, the entire meaning she gave to it, could be summed up in these words . . .

Yoo-Min lay helplessly on her yo as her mother's image disappeared into a blurry mist. Tears flowed from her almond eyes and soaked her pillowcase. From somewhere in her head, her mother's spectral voice came to her:

"You are beautiful, my darling."

Eyes softened with sorrow, Yoo-Min felt the fabulous warmth of her mother's love wash over her. She heard herself respond:

"I want to be the most beautiful girl in Korea."

"My dear, why would you want such a thing?"

"Because beauty is power. If I'm beautiful, everyone will love me."

"What a thought! How could you think this way, my daughter?"

"I'm so lonely, Mother. I want someone to love me and make me forget how lonely I am."

Loneliness was the essence of her existence. It permeated her life, filled every nook and cranny of her being like a wet, spongy fungus. Day and night, there was no escape from this loneliness. Sometimes her loneliness was so unbearable that she considered killing herself. But her fear of death was greater than the pain of living, and so she endured.

Yoo-Min prepared for her day in her usual fashion. Donning a pair of shorts and a loose-fitting tee shirt, she did her stretching exercises for half an hour. Her body was lithe and easily assumed the various positions required of it. When she finished, she was glistening with sweat.

Slipping effortlessly out of her clothes, she let them fall to the floor in a heap. Her smooth skin shone with youth and vim; her body positively radiated health. She walked across the room and into the bathroom, her small hips moving frugally, with an economy of effort usually found in much younger girls. The floor was cool against her bare soles. She turned on the faucet of the shower and set the temperature moderately hot. She pulled off the black elastic band holding her hair in a ponytail and tossed it on the floor outside the door.

Her shower was long and gratifying. The pulsing spray of hot water massaged her thoroughly, sinking deep into her pores and invigorating her completely. Afterwards, she dried herself and sat naked on the chair in front of her vanity.

From where she sat, she could see herself in the mirror that hung over the vanity. She studied herself critically. She was pleased by what she saw. She had to admit that even by her own impeccable standards her face was stunning. Her eyes were cold and intense, intimating an icy sensuality. Her nose was exquisitely shaped. Her lips were genuinely well-defined, which made her looks all the more striking. The only criticism she could muster was that her breasts were too small. Sufficiently ample breasts were important weapons in a woman's arsenal.

Stroking her thighs, she felt in her fingertips the pleasure they would bring to a man and a smile came to her lips. She prided herself on her ability to know her own strengths and weaknesses. Unfortunately, in her estimation, her weaknesses outnumbered her strengths. For one thing, she rued knowing that she was entirely dependent upon men. She needed a man's able shoulders to lean upon, someone as strong and solid as a rock, someone who would take care of her, which meant of course that he had to be financially secure.

"Someone like my father," she said aloud, reaching for a bottle of moisturizing lotion and rubbing a dab onto her leg. The cool balm soothed her skin.

Rising from her chair, she did a pirouette in front of the mirror and admired the long, graceful lines of her smooth back, the delicate curves of her small buttocks as they cast subtle shadows on her skin. She felt the latent power in her naked body and it gave her a confidence she otherwise would not have.

Staring vacantly at the ondol floor where her toes had left moist circlets, her thoughts turned to her father. Her father had died unexpectedly the year before. The sadness she felt upon her father's death was tempered by the knowledge that he had left behind a modest estate. With the money from her inheritance she was able to purchase brand new furniture. Her tastes were modern and expensive. She liked the sensuosity of material things and appreciated what money could buy. Money dulled the pain of her existence. She equated the numbness of her soul as something akin to happiness.

"I could never love a man who doesn't have money," she said to herself.

Pushing the hair from her eyes, she sang the words to a popular song:

> *Without money, love is gone;*
> *Love is money, it's the same;*
> *Without money, there is no love;*
> *Without money, love is gone, love is gone.*

Some time ago, she had come to the conclusion that there were three conditions a man must satisfy before she would allow herself to love him. At some point she had memorialized the list. In a writing tablet she had written these conditions in bold blue ink across the top of the opening page. The lines she scrawled were numbered one through three. Rummaging through the drawer of her vanity, she found the tablet and, flinging herself on her yo, read once again the conditions she had written:

1.   *He must be handsome.*

The image of Park Suk-Jun came to her mind and her head swam in a cloud of numb sensation. Suk-Jun was a rising star on television and adored by women young and old all over Korea. His handsome face graced the covers of all the popular entertainment magazines.

Contemplating Suk-Jun's looks, she took certain pleasure in drawing his picture with a lead pencil in the upper right hand corner of the tablet. When she finished, she pursed her lips tentatively and appraised her rendering with a critical eye. Her strokes were light and crude, but hadn't they effectively captured the essence of his good looks? She continued down the list:

2. *He must be rich.*

On that score, Suk-Jun was ideal. Not only was he a television sensation and female heartthrob to boot, but he came from an extremely wealthy family. His father was the chief of a giant chaebol. Moreover, she was sure his head wasn't cluttered with too many ideas. This would make him easy to control. She moved on to the next item:

3. *He must be a real man.*

She underscored Condition Number Three with her finger. She wanted a man who was strong and silent and sure of himself, a man who would ruthlessly make love to her every night. But he must be faithful to her as well. She couldn't bear the thought of a man having made it with another girl and then spreading his filth in her.

Biting her nail, she recalled what her best friend So-Yun had told her.

"Men can't be trusted," So-Yun had said, cynically. "And the ones who say they can are liars."

Yoo-Min frowned with the memory of this conversation. So-Yun had a disparaging view of men and their relationships with women. She believed that every man wanted a woman who was inferior in all respects, a woman who recognized that her place was always beneath a man's and whose primary function was to satisfy his turbulent desires. She remembered what So-Yun once had told her:

"Men are all alike. They'll sleep with any girl who'll give them half a chance. What do they know of love? They only know how to copulate." Laughing, So-Yun had added, "Men haven't the vaguest idea of what love is, yet how passionately they copulate!"

She detested her friend for those remarks. The idea of Suk-Jun having slept with dozens of other girls broke darkly into her thoughts.

"He's got a big jaji and he knows how to use it!"

"How do know that?"

"That's what all the girls say!"

She angrily crossed out the picture she had drawn with a flurry of pencil strokes. Flinging the tablet across the room, she watched dismally as its white pages fluttered like the broken wings of a dove before it slammed into the wall.

All day Yoo-Min shut herself in her room and would not dress or even fix herself something to eat. Benumbed with boredom and loneliness, she browsed through her collection of fashion magazines. There was nothing she saw that interested her. She didn't bother to read the articles.

For a while, she took satisfaction in painting her toenails. She found the task sufficiently mindless, though it required a modicum of concentration. Besides, she liked the color she had chosen: coral pink.

Several times she paced the room, but each time afterwards she was completely enervated and it was all she could do to crawl back onto her yo. Suffocating with emptiness, she wanted to die. But as she commenced to bite through her tongue so that she might bleed to death, the sharpness of her pain took her by surprise; she ceased her effort. Frustrated, she lay tormented by the thoughts that plagued her.

As it had in her thoughts, darkness crept little by little into her apartment. She read a few chapters of the roman à clef *Angmanun Prada-rul Ipnunda*. Around nine o'clock she consumed a light dinner, just a handful of rice and vegetables, and some soy milk to drink, while she watched her favorite television drama, the one starring Suk-Jun. When it was over, she went online and logged onto Cyworld to visit Suk-Jun's minihompy. Suk-Jun's avatar, a gnome-like creature in a long, flowing robe, the garb of his television character, gazed at her with the dark, brooding eyes of a troubled soul, a disenchanted romantic perhaps. She read his blog and saw that he was on location filming in Chungcheongnam-do. She posted a message in the visitor's book. It began: *Dearest Suk-Jun, I am your biggest fan.* Her message was brief and shorn of the gushing adoration of his younger fans.

After awhile her heart grew quiet, but the black pall that had descended upon her thoughts would not go away. Through the window of her room she watched as the lights of Seoul danced in the darkness. She felt a stabbing in her breast, caught up as she was in the complexity of her emotions.

Finally, beset with weariness, she lay on her yo and shut her eyes and slipped lightly into unconsciousness. Behind her closed eyes, indistinct phantasms rose up. Her grandmother, long since dead, wafted up before her only to disappear moments later. Aunts and uncles she had known in life both remotely and intimately came and went without a sign. Then her mother appeared, full of life and marvelously beautiful. Seeing her mother, pangs of sadness cut at her like blades of swords, and without knowing it, her cheeks became stained with tears.

She had a dream. It did not feel like a dream to her. She was lying on her yo. A heavy silence hung in the air. The room seemed empty but the hackles on her neck informed her that it was not.

She was suddenly cognizant of someone hovering over her. How was this possible? She felt his eyes upon her, caressing her ever so softly with them but without touching her. Before she could move or make any sound whatsoever, he descended upon her light as leaves and closer than air. She wanted to shriek with terror, but the sound caught in her throat like a wounded bird and was strangled there. Somewhere in a faraway place in her mind, she heard a voice shout, *Wake up. It's only a dream.* She had the vague realization that life itself was a dream. And then, as the voice faded into a shrill silence, she felt his jaji probing her thighs, while through the window she could see rose-colored lances thrust themselves above the skyscrapers of Seoul, up into the morning sky.

Not too many days later, Kwang-Chul sat at a table by the window in Glade listening to kayageum music and drinking hot bori-cha while munching on kimchi and reading from a book of hyangga. He read them not in the modern hangul, but in the hyangch'al style of Chinese writing.

It was early evening and Glade was just opening for business. A solitary patron, a young businessman decked out in a single-breasted, three-piece suit, sat in a booth with its purple velvet curtains partially open, drinking from a half-empty bottle of soju with a pretty, sloe-eyed hostess cooing at his side. In another booth, two miniskirted hostesses assiduously applied their makeup. Chan-Woo, Glade's bartender, stood behind the bar polishing Hite beer glasses. Kwang-Chul's mother was busy in the kitchen preparing a variety of side dishes that Glade served. The pungent smell of garlic, onions, and hot chili peppers filled the premises.

Outside the sun stretched itself across the evening sky, looking very much like a flattened orange.

Kwang-Chul's thoughts were like the approaching night sky, clear and untroubled. True, in closing the book on his lap, he wistfully rued the fact that a collection of hyangga compiled during the reign of Queen Chinsŏng by the monk Taegu had been lost, but this was such a fleeting lament that it did nothing to disturb the quiet contentment he felt.

Kwang-Chul was enthralled by the sheer beauty of the hyangga. He believed that the capacity to appreciate beauty was the mark of a superior individual. Only the truly elite could feel the pull and sway of something that was at once both an idea and an object of some palpability. No one he knew appreciated beauty the way he did. Their hearts were

41

not set aflame as was his, they did not burn with a fire that was almost holy in its zeal to consume their souls. When others looked upon beauty, they did not feel, as did he, that nothing else mattered – not work, not filial piety, not loyalty to one's country, not even life itself.

Contemplating the beauty of the hyangga, a marvelous luminosity shone in his thoughts, breaking through the inveterate darkness which always defined his world.

As the waning sunlight filtering through the plate glass window produced a mottled pattern on the pages of his book, he thought:

How can I explain the feeling that comes over me whenever I'm in the presence of beauty? There's a fire in my heart that renders all other fires pale and lifeless, a fire that doesn't consume but rather exalts me. Its flames aren't the insipid flames of a miserable, squalid passion, a shabby lust conceived in the flesh, but the incandescent flames of a higher yearning, an unmistakably supernal longing. In moments like these, I feel the fierce passion of my soul, the violent longing in me for what is divine in the universe, a longing so far above the crude, vulgar desires of a man as the stars are above the earth.

His eyes flashed with unaccustomed happiness. His gaze meandered from the pair of stylishly sleek hostesses who were powdering their faces sop-white and touching up their painted ruby lips to a fountain outside in the center of a small plaza across the street, where columns of hazy white water shot upwards and outwards, then hurled themselves fearlessly into a pool below; to the dark-drenched buildings of Seoul towering above the skyline; to a group of powdery-faced girls in navy blue school uniforms who were passing in front of Glade, giggling among themselves; to the fountain again, where the jetting columns of water straining to reach the heavens failed gloriously in their quest, instead spraying the air with misty droplets that descended like snowflakes and melted at the fountain's pearly base; to the delicate purple gauze that had unraveled itself across a surrealistic sky.

The entire scene, observed piecemeal but assimilated as a whole far greater than the sum of its myriad parts, imbued him with a feeling of tranquility and intimacy with creation.

Succumbing to an extraordinary illusion, he felt as if the whole universe was revolving around a central point, the very spot in Glade where he had chosen to sit.

Everything seemed like a shimmering piece of unreality, like the tapestry of a dream.

The next thing he knew: *she* walked into Glade. He could scarcely believe his eyes.

It's her! The girl from my dream! She's real!

Lowering his lashes, he watched her surreptitiously. Etched against the purple-glutted sky, she seemed strangely unreal to him, as if she belonged to another world altogether. Yet he was convinced that somehow, in some inexplicable way, she had made herself known to him, had drawn him into the orbit of her existence. Or was it the mournful strains of the kayageum which tugged at his soul? The juxtaposition of girl and kayageum, the beguiling strains of another time and place, the sultry summer night outside, the coruscating stars, and vague feelings of déjà vu – surely there was something auspicious in the air. She glanced his way and for the briefest moment her eyes lingered on his. He pondered the subtle intimations of his destiny.

She was astonishingly beautiful. Her face was thin and sensitive and as white as a sculpted pearl brooch he had once seen in a jewelry shop. It floated before his eyes in the murky light like a pale scepter. Her lips were flawless, teeming with a blustery sensuality. They complimented her perfectly shaped nose. He thought that the artist who had given shape to this vision of womanhood had completely mastered the elements of space, light, and shadow.

Her eyes were shining and proud. They suggested to him an idealistic nature, but one tethered to the earth. He felt his stomach knot with excitement as he contemplated the shafts of light emanating from her eyes. Here was a girl who could give substance to his dreams. The smile on her face was luminous and threatened to dispel the usual sense of isolation that engulfed him.

Only in some distant reality, or in death perhaps, had he thought that such remarkable beauty could exist.

His sensations were aroused to the utmost degree. It seemed to him that the progression of events compelling him to this moment in time and this point in space, the girl's beauty and the potential of the night, were all proof of the subtle orchestrations of the universe. Surely the sounds of the kayageum were cajoling him now, coaxing him to do what on any other night would be the unthinkable. His mind screamed: *Take a chance! What have you got to lose but your entire future?*

He envisioned himself shamelessly going up to her and baring his soul as he had never done before. He imagined that she would listen to him, and that, persuaded by his sincerity, she would open up her heart to him. He felt the pride swell up in him when he thought of the words he would present to her as gifts of love: *I've always dreamed of being with a girl just like you. But I've always thought that a girl like you existed only in my dreams.*

But he did nothing of the sort. As luck would have it, just then a terrifically handsome fellow strolled into Glade and lit up a cigarette. Kwang-Chul recognized him immediately: Park Suk-Jun, the television actor and son of one of the richest men in Seoul. Suk-Jun had the looks of real lady-killer.

He saw that the girl had spotted Suk-Jun. She perceptibly stiffened, a sure sign that Suk-Jun had piqued her interest. Worse than that, she threw Kwang-Chul a glance that told him in no uncertain terms: *Don't be ridiculous. I could never be interested in you.*

Flushed with embarrassment, Kwang-Chul lowered his head and pretended that he was reading. He prayed fervently that Suk-Jun wouldn't notice the girl. But Suk-Jun had already seen her and was appraising her with the same cool eye as one might appraise an expensive gem through a jeweler's loupe. Suk-Jun's eyes seemed to lewdly say: *This girl's fantastic. Just once, I'd like to get my hands on her breasts and feel their splendid, palpable softness. I won't be satisfied until I've done so.*

And then, spotting Kwang-Chul, those same eyes coagulated into a sudden firmness. Suk-Jun casually blew a smoke ring into the air, as if to say, *She's mine.* The band of smoke enlarged itself like an ethereal proteus and drifted lazily away.

With a contemptuous smile, Suk-Jun threw down his cigarette and rubbed it out with the sole of his shoe. He walked up to the table where the girl sat. She was mindlessly playing with her long hair.

"Mind if I join you?"

The girl flashed an alluring smile. Her teeth gleamed like freshwater pearls.

"Not at all."

"I'm Park Suk-Jun."

"I know! You're my favorite actor! I can't believe it's really you!"

Suk-Jun smiled handsomely. "You must be Yoo-Min. I've been reading your posts on my Cyworld page."

"Omigod! You know who I am? But how did you know I'd be here?"

Listening to every word, Kwang-Chul watched in dismay as the smile on Suk-Jun's face widened into a shark-toothed grin. "How else? Fate brought me here."

"But how'd you know it's me?"

"I'd recognize you anywhere."

From the doorway to the kitchen, Kim Kyung-A suddenly appeared. She impatiently signaled Kwang-Chul to take care of them.

Kwang-Chul cursed his miserable luck. He would rather die than wait on the girl while she was with Suk-Jun. Burying his head in his book, he tried in vain to focus on the hyangch'al wavering on its pages, all the while praying fervently that his mother would disappear into the kitchen and remain there. But Kyung-A had no intention of doing so.

"Quit dawdling!" she bellowed, wagging a sauce-stained finger at him.

He sullenly slammed his book shut and shuffled over to the table where the girl and Suk-Jun sat cozily admiring each other. Tossing down a pair of menus, he faked a dumb smile while Suk-Jun picked one up and scanned it from cover to cover. The girl ignored the other menu completely. She said:

"Boshintang."

"It's not on the menu."

"Eh? What do you mean?"

"We don't sell boshintang."

"I want boshintang," she said, glaring at him.

Kwang-Chul squirmed uncomfortably as a strand of saliva stretching between her parted chrysanthemum lips glistened like silk thread. With a throb of ecstasy, he thought that he could die for such a mouth. He ruefully mused: *Now why did she have to want boshintang? It would have been better had she just kept her mouth shut!*

"But they don't sell it," said Suk-Jun placatingly. "Besides, I don't like dog meat."

"I don't care," she said. "I want it."

As if that settled the matter, she turned her attention to a speck of dried-up food on the table and flicked at it with her fingernail.

"It's illegal," Kwang-Chul told both of them. "Please select something else."

Just then his mother appeared at his side looking as fresh as a spring blossom. "What's the problem here?"

"We want boshintang," said the girl, putting on a marvelous sulk.

"It's the dog days," Suk-Jun said, shrugging. Smiling handsomely at Kwang-Chul's mother, he added, "You understand."

Kwang-Chul threw his mother a severe look. "I was just explaining that we don't sell boshintang. I asked them to choose something else."

"Nonsense!" said Kyung-A, placing a hand on the sleeve of Suk-Jun's dragon-embroidered silk shirt. "Of course we sell boshintang!"

"What!" Kwang-Chul almost spat out his teeth in amazement.

"You understand that we must be careful," said Kyung-A with a wink at Suk-Jun. She gave Kwang-Chul a jab with her elbow.

He flinched as the girl shot him a smug look that said, *I told you so.*

"It'll take time, though," said Kyung-A, flashing her pearl-white teeth at Suk-Jun. "But I guarantee you, it'll be worth the wait!"

Whirling on her heels, she sashayed her way to the kitchen. Kwang-Chul nearly pulled out his hair – the shapely calves of his mother's legs were discernible through the slit in her skirt, a sight he was sure was not lost upon that roué Suk-Jun.

As if to exacerbate things, the girl knocked the menus off the table. He was sure it was deliberate. In a voice dripping with mock civility, she said to him, "Oh, boy? Would you mind picking those up?"

Silently fuming, he snatched up the menus and stalked after his mother. Kyung-A stood in front of a counter marinating slices of beef in soy sauce for pulgogi when he entered the kitchen.

Slamming down the menus, he snapped angrily, "I can't believe the way you were fawning over that cow's ass like a whore from one of the kisaeng houses!"

Kyung-A paid him no mind. "Idiot! Don't you know who that is? He's rich! He'll spend a lot of money here!"

"Who does that girl think she is ordering boshintang like that? Maybe she's with the police. Anyway, what's her game coming in here and bamboozling our customers?"

"Don't be stupid. She's not the police. That's Yoo-Min. She's our new hostess."

"What? Why wasn't I told? Don't I have any say around here?"

"You? What do you know about such things? Don't be an ass! That girl's different; she's not like the others. With looks like hers, she'll make a bundle for us!"

48

"That guy has all the luck!" Kwang-Chul rued, idly picking up a stainless steel pot lid and examining his reflection on the surface of its underside. His oval-shaped face resembled a cratered moon. "He waltzes in here and gets the most beautiful girl just like that! And why? It's only because he's good-looking, famous, and rich. What girl wouldn't go for a guy like that?"

"Can you blame her?"

"And did you see his hair?" Kwang-Chul ran his hand through his thinning hair. "What a fantastic head of hair! Damn, what I wouldn't give to have hair like that!"

Kyung-A grabbed a dirty wet rag and threw it at his head. Her aim was off and the rag hit the wall behind him with a resounding slap, but a fish head that had been wrapped up in the rag followed a different trajectory and caught him in the neck.

"What are you talking about? I know what you're thinking! You're such a dreamer! What would a beautiful girl like her want with someone like you?"

Kwang-Chul angrily picked up the fish head and flipped it onto the counter. He complained bitterly, "We haven't any boshintang. You know that. Now what are we going to do?"

"Quit whining!" Kyung-A snapped at him. She tossed the fish head into a simmering pot of spicy fish stew. "Think of something! Use that bald head of yours! You always have it buried in a book. It must be good for something!"

"I'll bet there isn't another girl like her in all of Seoul," he rued wistfully, casting his eye on the pot of fish stew. He bent over the pot and inhaled deeply. Savoring the pungent aroma, he sighed, "Why can't I have a girl like that? Did you see her eyes? They're finer than black sapphires!"

Kyung-A scratched her head as she thought furiously. Her eyes were as black as those of a freshwater shrimp. "Wait a minute! I have an idea!"

"What's that?"

"You know that restaurant around the corner? The one with the red lantern in front?"

"Sure."

"The owner has a jindo he keeps tied up outside!"

"So?"

"Are you stupid? Get that dog and bring it back here! We'll have boshintang, alright!"

"But it's not yellow dog," protested Kwang-Chul.

"Who cares? It's still dog."

Kwang-Chul gazed admiringly at his mother. Arms akimbo and eyes blazing like fire arrows, she resembled an indefatigable, unbeatable warrior preparing to mount an attack on the flank of an unsuspecting enemy. Such a brilliant idea! Yes, they would have boshintang soon enough! One jindo coming up! And best of all, it would impress Yoo-Min when he served her fresh, steaming boshintang!

"What are you standing around for, lazy-bones? Get to it!" Kyung-A ordered, banging the pot with a metal ladle.

"You mean me?"

"Who else?"

Kwang-Chul looked sorrily at his feet and blushed a cherry blossom red. "I hate dogs," he said.

Kyung-A craned her neck as if she hadn't heard him correctly. "What are you talking about?"

"They give me the creeps."

"Don't be a silly ass! Get that dog! You want to impress that girl out there, don't you?"

"I'll be right back!" Kwang-Chul cried, saluting his mother.

"Wait! Take this!"

With a sharp cutting knife, Kyung-A sliced off a large piece of sausage stuffed with beef intestines, rice, garlic, ginger and beef blood. She lobbed it to Kwang-Chul, who stuffed it in his shirt pocket.

Kwang-Chul bolted out the back door. Half a dozen shops lined the narrow street behind Glade, their bright neon signs advertising a variety of fare: barbecued meat, bibimpap, noodles and dumplings, soon dubu, and other specialty foods. From the drinking houses that offered inexpensive soju, makkoli, and dongdongju came the boisterous sounds of revelry. At either end of the street, vendors sold clams, squid, oysters, and kimchi to passersby from portable tents illuminated by carbide lamps. A group of university students stumbled drunkenly through the street, shouting and cursing and laughing all at once.

"Sung-Hi, are you cold? Let me warm you up!"

"Get your filthy hands off me, Chan-Sung!"

"Come on, I just want to warm you."

"I told you, don't touch me!"

"Where shall we eat?"

"How about that place? Glade."

"Are you crazy? The food there's terrible!"

Several of the group were tall, willowy young women with shining faces and long spidery legs who, on any other night, would give Kwang-Chul pause. But on this particular night he passed them by without as much as a glance. All he could think about was Yoo-Min waiting for her boshintang and that devil Suk-Jun waiting for his opportunity.

He found the jindo precisely where his mother said it would be – tied up in front of the restaurant with the red lantern. Down the street from the restaurant, an old man was drunkenly staggering. A stone's toss away, three middle-aged businessmen perched on wooden stools in front a street vendor's food stall eating bean cakes and galbi and drinking makkoli while they chatted among themselves. Kwang-Chul slipped quietly past them and approached the white-haired jindo cautiously.

"Here, poochie!"

He sank into a crouch and held out his hand. The jindo bounded to its feet and bared its teeth with a snarl. "Easy, poochie," said Kwang-Chul soothingly, yanking his hand away. "I'm not going to hurt you." He eyed the jindo warily and thought: *Just wait till I get my hands on you! I'm going to wring your neck!*

Pulling out the sausage that dangled from his shirt pocket, he tore off a piece and tossed it to the jindo. The dog ate it greedily. When it finished, it licked its chops and dumbly wagged its tail.

"That's right," he said, flipping it another piece of sausage. "Come and get it!"

"Hey, what's going on here?"

Kwang-Chul looked up, startled. He thought it was the jindo's owner. But it was the drunken old man.

"Nothing, buddy. Just go on your way."

"What's that? Who do you think you are? Show some respect!"

"Get out of here! Shoo!" Kwang-Chul was afraid the old drunk would attract someone's attention. He glanced anxiously at the businessmen sitting by the street vendor's tent but they were engrossed in conversation.

"I won't!"

"What do you mean? Get away from here, I say!"

The old drunk swayed like a bamboo tree in a strong wind.

"What are you doing with that dog?"

"None of your business."

"I know what you're up to! You're going to take her home and eat her! You can't do that! That's Joo-Joo! She's a favorite around here. I won't let you eat Joo-Joo!"

"Don't be an idiot! I'm not going to eat her," insisted Kwang-Chul as the dog sniffed his shoes. "I'm just feeding her."

"Not going to eat her? Then why are you feeding her? Fattening her up for the slaughter, I'd say! You're up to something!"

With that, the old drunk stepped forward to intervene, but with his first step he lost his balance and crumpled to the ground. Sitting on his rump, he began wailing, "Joo-Joo! He's going to eat poor Joo-Joo!"

Kwang-Chul's temper rose. He hissed at the old drunk, "Shut up, you inebriated fool!" Just then he noticed a suspicious stain on the old drunk's pants. "Say, what have you done to yourself?"

"Eh?"

"Your pants. You've pissed in them."

The old drunk looked down at his pants. "Aw," he moaned, crestfallen. "I pissed in my pants." His face brightened. "I'm not the only one, ha, ha!"

Kwang-Chul looked down to see the jindo pissing on his leg. "Hey, get out of here, you dumb mutt! What's the big idea?"

"Karma," guffawed the old drunk, slapping his thigh.

Kwang-Chul ignored him. He threw the jindo several more pieces of sausage and by this means slowly won the dog's confidence. He looked over his shoulder and saw that the old drunk had curled up on the street and fallen asleep. Undoing the rope, he led the jindo away and brought it back to Glade, but not before he had given the old man a kick in the seat of his pants. "Drunken bastard," he muttered, jindo in tow.

"Take it into the storage room," his mother commanded upon his return. "And be quick about it."

He coaxed the jindo into the storage room and flipped on the light. He ordered the dog to sit. It stupidly obeyed. Reaching for an old hickory cane that stood upright in a corner of the room, he cautiously advanced on the jindo. Suspecting that something was up, the dog growled uneasily. In the style of a bong sul fighter, Kwang-Chul fell into an attack stance. Inhaling on the move, he stepped forward and raised the cane over his head. His right hand tightened around the cane. Lowering his center of gravity and exhaling with the strike, he brought the cane within striking distance of the jindo's muzzle – and checked his blow.

Kyung-A poked her head into the room. "How's it coming? I have the kettle boiling!"

His face drooped apologetically. "I can't."

Kyung-A looked at him incredulously. "What's wrong with you? Give me that!" She snatched the cane from his hand, glaring at him scornfully. "And you call yourself a man?"

She cracked the cane over the jindo's head. The jindo let out a yelp and crumpled to the floor. Blood and foam spewed from its mouth, staining the floor peppermint red. Its stunned eyes looked up at her as if to ask, *Why?*

"See, that's how it's done!" she cried exultantly. She threw him a look of smug satisfaction. "A child could do it!" She fixed her gaze on the jindo. "Take that!"

54

She brought the cane down a second time. The jindo's ribs cracked like the mast of a ship snapping in two. "And that! And that!" She struck the jindo again and again, bringing the animal closer to death with each blow, but each blow carefully aimed so as not to deliver it from its torment. There was still life in its glazed eyes.

"It won't do to kill it just yet!" she cried. "You need to beat it awhile to tenderize the meat!"

Her face glistened feverishly in the dull yellow glow of an overhanging light bulb. Sweating from her labor, she worked the brute over methodically. But the excitement of the kill proved too much for her – her blows soon rained down upon the jindo with such a fury that nothing would have been left of the beast but a pulp had Kwang-Chul not stayed her hand. The bloody mess on the floor was unrecognizable as a jindo.

"What have you done to that poor thing?" he asked, horrified.

"Quit your blubbering," she said, tossing him the cane. "And get me a carving knife!"

Later, when the boshintang was ready, Kyung-A brought it out in a steaming iron pot and set it on the table in the booth where Yoo-Min and Suk-Jun were sitting like a pair of star-crossed lovers.

"Soup's on!"

"Excellent!" proclaimed Yoo-Min, sniffing the boshintang with delight.

Kyung-A spooned out two large bowls and set them in front of the pair. Suk-Jun gamely dipped a spoon into his bowl and tasted its contents. He graciously smacked his lips.

"You're right! It was worth the wait!"

Kyung-A beamed proudly and withdrew from the booth. Kwang-Chul lingered nearby on some pretext, pretending not to notice the couple but making sure to hear every word that passed between them.

"Great night, isn't it?" asked Suk-Jun, picking with a toothpick at a piece of jindo stuck between his teeth.

"Yes, it's incredible."

"You know, there's something about this night I just can't explain. There's something amazing, perhaps even miraculous about this night. Why, a night like this probably only comes once a century or so."

"You think so?"

"Absolutely. But it's not just the night, mind you. To tell you the truth, I've never seen a girl like you before. I'm sure I met you for a purpose."

Kwang-Chul's ears were burning. He could scarcely believe what he was hearing. *Those are my lines! He's saying just what I wanted to say!*

"I feel the same way," said Yoo-Min, fluttering her lashes.

Confused, and at a sudden loss for what to do, Kwang-Chul gazed through the window at the night sky outside. Overhead, the stars were signaling in undecipherable code. Kwang-Chul stared hard at the points of glittering light and tried to discern their meaning, but he saw only chaos and uncertainty.

"What's wrong? Are you alright?"

The stars receded into the fabric of the night. Kwang-Chul heard Suk-Jun choking on a piece of jindo behind him. He turned to see Yoo-Min pounding frantically on Suk-Jun's back. For one mad, glorious moment, Kwang-Chul's heart soared with joy as he wildly thought:

Good for you! Choke! Die!

"Sweet dreams, dear."

Listening in the dark as his mother's footsteps receded from the door, Kwang-Chul waited until he was sure that she was no longer in the vicinity of his room.

Moving quietly, he unfastened his belt and slipped out of his jeans. All evening he had been itching for bed and now that the time had come he could scarcely control himself.

"If only I can dream of her again," he said to himself, yanking off his socks and tossing them on the floor. He scowled resentfully as he felt the hard ondol floor against the soles of his bare feet. As it always did, reality stood as a formidable barrier between him and the attainment of his desires.

He couldn't get Yoo-Min out of his mind. All night long he had been thinking about her and nothing else. No matter how hard he tried to concentrate on other things, she was always there, lurking in the back of his mind, an untouchable mental picture bathed in an unearthly purity.

Even his conversation with Chan-Woo earlier that night on the famous Four-Seven debate had failed to dislodge her from his thoughts. This seemed all the more remarkable to him since the Four-Seven debate was by far and away the most renowned philosophical controversy in Korean history.

This famous argument had started when Yi Hwang stated that the Four Beginnings – humanity, righteousness, propriety, and wisdom – were the effluence of principle, whereas the Seven Feelings – pleasure, anger, sorrow, worry, fear, desire, and joy – were the issuance of material force. Moreover, Yi Hwang had argued, the Four Beginnings were good, whereas the Seven Feelings could sometimes be good

57

and sometimes evil. Ki Taesŭng disagreed. How could the Seven Feelings not be good? If the Seven Feelings were the issuance of material force, then they must be something external to principle. But what can be external to principle? Ki Taesŭng reasoned that if the Seven Feelings cannot be external to principle, they themselves must be the effluence of principle and therefore they must be good.

"A point," Kwang-Chul said excitedly, wagging a finger at Chan-Woo, who was busy stuffing his face with bean cake at the time, "that Yi I convincingly argued in his letter to Sŏng Hon a decade later. For if principle and material force are to be separated, then even yin and yang would have a commencement. Consequently, the Seven Feelings *must* be consubstantial with the Four Beginnings. Can you see this?" To which Chan-Woo, utterly bewildered, nonetheless obligingly responded with his mouth full of bean cake and crumbs dribbling down his chin. "I see! I see!" And Kwang-Chul himself began to see the glimmer of a fantastic notion formulating in his mind.

Later, with scattered remnants of this discussion still permeating his brain, he had trudged upstairs to his room over Glade. It was then that an exciting idea burst into his head. Could it be that Yoo-Min and the impossible happiness he sought were of the same shimmering substance?

Shutting his eyes, he focused upon Yoo-Min's image in his thoughts: her long, flowing black hair; her lips which resembled plucked berries bursting with maturity; the impeccable softness of her pallid skin; the delicious warmth that flowed from deep within her flesh like sun-soaked honey.

His recollection of her was a powerful one. Details he normally would have forgotten had not been effaced by the passage of time. He held her image faithfully in his thoughts, while his mind turned to the moment he had first lain eyes upon her. Everything about that moment seemed unreal, existing as mere abstraction, as things always did whenever he seemed poised on the verge of a miraculous discovery . . .

"To hell with you!"

Kwang-Chul flung open his eyes and hurled his pillow across the room. It sailed over the figurine of the Pongsan masked dancer and smacked soundlessly against the wall.

It irked him to know that Yoo-Min hadn't showed the slightest interest in him. Why couldn't she see at a glance that he was special? Why couldn't she sense his uniqueness as surely as any dumb animal could sense an approaching thunderstorm? Couldn't she feel his potential sizzling beneath his skin like an egg frying on a hot skillet? Couldn't she understand that he was someone who could do just about anything with his life, if he put his mind to it?

He could feel fate singling him out, testing his mettle, measuring his worth, judging whether he was a man capable of fulfilling its inscrutable plans.

Tossing restlessly on his sweat-soaked mattress, he recalled how his spirits had turned pitch black when he watched Yoo-Min and Suk-Jun leave Glade and walk arm-in-arm into the night. Suk-Jun had glanced back over his shoulder and thrown him a derisive look that said, *She'll never be yours. Never.*

Burying his face in his sheet, he commenced once again to scrutinize Yoo-Min as he remembered how she looked that night. She had been wearing a sleeveless, black matte dress with spaghetti straps joined at the neckline. Her neck was long and regal and formed a smooth continuity with her shoulders. Gently sloping, her shoulders insinuated pleasure. He envisioned himself standing behind her and firmly holding them with his face softly nuzzled against the nape of her neck. . . .

Waking up, Yoo-Min knew that she had been troubled by an odd dream. She could not remember what her dream had been about, but she had the vaguest recollection that it had disturbed her. Lying on her yo with her right hand pressed against her pillow, she felt unusually heavy and dull, as if a paralysis had descended upon her while she slept. She wriggled her toes and twisted her fingers to test the sensation in them. They felt fine. Satisfied, she decided that there was no cause for worry.

Several times she seemed on the verge of remembering a particular aspect of her dream, but each time she was unable to bring into the light of consciousness the murky images which lay just beneath the surface of her awareness. Each time she closed her eyes and wrinkled her forehead to force them to submit to her scrutiny, but in spite of her best efforts her memory faltered, and the images she endeavored to dredge up from the depths of her unconsciousness fell back into the shadowy unreality from whence they came.

But even more troubling than the dream she could not recollect was the distinct feeling that someone had been in her room while she slept. Tingling deep within her flesh was the uncomfortable knowledge that a man's eyes had absorbed her nakedness while she slept – eyes that had glimmered with unmistakable pleasure.

Or had *this* been her dream? Mulling it over, she could not decide one way or the other. When So-Yun called on the phone moments later, she described her concerns.

"Perhaps it wasn't a dream," she told her friend.

"What else could it be?"

"I don't know. Maybe someone was in my bedroom."

61

"But who?" So-Yun's voice was alarmed.

"I don't know," she said nervously.

"I'm sure it was just a dream." So-Yun's voice suddenly sounded hollow and disinterested. "I wouldn't worry about it if I were you."

"Then it was a very strange dream," Yoo-Min said softly.

Hanging up, she closed her eyes and felt the world press upon her with its immensity; the closeness of her surroundings, the inescapable weight of the present moment, filled her heart with bewildering emotions.

Drifting in and out of sleep, thoughts about Suk-Jun came to her. She was moist with sweat and her head ached with longing and uncertainty. Why wasn't he with her now? Why wasn't he holding her in his arms? These questions shrieked in her heart like the shrills of a wild beast.

She had met Suk-Jun the night before. In no time at all she discovered that the attraction between them, like the irresistible pull of opposing magnetic poles, was too powerful to ignore.

Broad and muscular, Suk-Jun appeared as if he had been molded out of some hard, metallic alloy. Even his eyes had the glint of dull copper. He reminded her of a heroic statue she had once seen in a museum.

Best of all, Suk-Jun was a flashy dresser. He wore expensive, brand name clothes and a solid gold chain and medallion around his neck. His fingernails were clipped and clean, while his shoes were so painstakingly polished that they reflected the least bit of ambient light. No doubt about it, Suk-Jun resembled a finely sculpted work of art.

Exultation filled Yoo-Min's heart as she contemplated Suk-Jun's fabulous looks. Nothing was more important to her than appearances. She could accept many faults, such as pride or vanity, but there were specific weaknesses she refused to indulge in, as they were tantamount to unpardonable sins – such as permitting herself to love someone who was not good looking. In her mind, beauty and goodness were one. She told herself:

Suk-Jun has the face of a god. How could he possibly have any faults?

The night before Suk-Jun had casually slipped his arm around her. His strong shoulders subsumed hers, and her supple, tender body seemed to sink naturally into the space under his arm. Like an oyster in a shell, she thought at the time.

Raising herself on her pillow, she sighed, "Suk-Jun isn't like all the others. How could he be?"

She was convinced that someone as marvelously attractive as Suk-Jun must possess a sensitivity akin to her own.

Thinking of Suk-Jun, she envisioned the sea. His waters were calm and deep, boundless, yet clear like his intentions. She could discern in those waters an immense power; it pulled at her like the lure of the sea that tugs at a sailor's heart.

She hugged her pillow tightly as she recalled how Suk-Jun's eyes had looked at her: large, doleful eyes, imponderably deep, eyes which did not waver but which held her face steadily in its gaze, a gaze so strong and sure and telling her in no uncertain terms, *I want you more than anything in the world.* She could not match that gaze second for second and had to avert her eyes. The strength of Suk-Jun's desire for her took her breath away.

He had taken her to a love hotel in It'aewon-dong. She felt a thrill when she remembered how he had kissed her – a full, deep, sensuous kiss, a kiss that would seal their love stronger than words. But when he tried to take things further, she had been adamant in her refusal.

"Don't touch me," she said coolly, pushing him away. She had had a sudden change of heart. She was a virgin and she intended to keep it that way.

Had she been wrong to refuse him? She had seen the disappointment in his face, the slight stiffening of his shoulders. At the time, she thought that she had hurt him a little, doubtless had wounded his pride. She was sure that he had completely misunderstood her – wouldn't that be typical of a man?

She was wide-awake now and her heart seemed to beat a little faster. She looked cautiously around the room, satisfying herself that no one was present – why should there be? Possessed by a sudden urge, she said in a voice scarcely above a whisper:

"Love me, Suk-Jun."

No sooner had the words escaped her lips than she was overcome with an intense yearning. Flinging back her ibul, she cried out:

"Love me, Suk-Jun! Love me! Love me!"

Trembling with desire, her eyes flashed brightly. The iron bars that had caged her heart for so long instantly vanished.

But then, casting her gaze about, she discerned the emptiness of her room. Wishing that Suk-Jun was with her, and realizing he was not, sadness once again encroached upon her tired heart.

Yoo-Min felt the life rush out of her limbs. The suffocating emptiness of the morning stirred her emotions to a feverish pitch. A feeling of dizziness overcame her and she thought that she would black out. She lay motionless, struggling to contain the tormenting emotions that threatened to extinguish her spirit.

She blamed her mood on the fact that her period was overdue. At last she decided that a new ensemble or piece of jewelry would cheer her up.

Mustering her energy, she dragged herself off her yo and stretched for twenty minutes. Afterwards she showered and toweled herself dry. Then she massaged an herbal emollient into her skin, vigorously rubbing her thighs to bring out the color in them and gently kneading her breasts until they were tender and screaming for a man's touch.

Next, she invested considerable time in the application of her makeup. Every brush stroke and line drawn had to be carefully considered and painstakingly applied to achieve maximum effect – the enhancement of her beauty was a rendering of both craft and art. She painted her lips with a fetching cherry wine lipstick as the final touch.

Standing in front of the mirror, she wondered what to do with her hair. She could go for a conservative look and knot it into a bun and pin it down with a rhinestone barrette. But that didn't suit her fancy at all. After some deliberation she opted for a feral look. She let her hair hang down tangled and wild like that of a savage mountain cat. Then she put on a fashionable ultra-short skirt that nipped at her buttocks and a shocking pink sheer blouse that clung to her small breasts like cellophane to fresh strawberries. She followed it up with a pair of dangling silver flute earrings and a platinum toe ring.

Every few seconds she observed herself in the mirror, rotating on her heels to see herself from every angle and paying rapt attention to the most scant detail, determined not to miss a trick. She was intent upon creating an image that no man could resist.

She caught the train at Yeouido station and later transferred to the number four line at Ch'ungmoro, arriving at Myeong-dong station just before noon. Stepping from the station into the street, her senses reeled from the heat and the humidity. It was one of those sweltering, festering days towards the end of July when the air was humid and thick like egg drop soup.

The city sizzled under a brutal sun. As usual, traffic was bumper-to-bumper and at a standstill. Drivers honked their horns in a cacophony of impatience. The sidewalks were bustling with activity. Scores of males and females of all shapes, sizes, and ages pushed and collided haphazardly against each other like molecules jiggling in thermal motion. Not a single face bore the slightest expression of apology.

Walking among the crowd, Yoo-Min felt the stares of the males who passed by her in their dark business suits. Dripping with sweat, they leered at her openly, sizing her up and ripping off her clothes with their eyes and fondling her in their thoughts. She was secretly pleased at the stir she had created.

Myeong-dong was a place where Yoo-Min went whenever she wanted to kill some time. She loved to shop in its fashion boutiques and famous department stores. On this particular morning, she spent the better part of two hours in one of the department stores trying on several women's suits, but found none to her liking. She passed another hour in the shoe department where she couldn't decide between a pair of Gucci loafers or Prada ankle boots. She moved on to women's accessories. To ease her growing sense of frustration, she settled on a black Gucci handbag with a silver clasp. She also purchased a white flacon bottle of *Zen Summer*, the new limited edition by Shiseido, a fragrance of blue rose and lotus that was just the scent for the dog days of summer.

Afterwards, she leisurely browsed through the jewelry section and tried on a one-and-a-half marquise cut diamond in a platinum six-prong solitaire setting. She fell in love with the ring immediately, but the diamond wasn't big enough. The size of the diamond was, in her mind, the truest measure of a man's love. She told herself with a smile: *Size matters.*

Leaving the department store, she decided to seek refuge in the teashop where So-Yun worked. There she could savor her small victories. Meandering through the side streets, she came upon it in no time. A sign in the window read: *Discover what the future holds for you. Have your fortune told here. Satisfaction guaranteed.*

The teashop was pleasant enough. Setting her bags on the floor, she took a seat in an antique elm wood chair in front of a low black and gold lacquered table by the window. There were no other patrons in the shop. So-Yun rushed up to greet her.

"Yoo-Min! I'm surprised to see you here!"

"I was in the area. I thought I'd stop by."

"Would you like something to drink?"

So-Yun had shoulder length hair, a gelatin-smooth face, and breasts like jade king melons. She was wearing a summer ramie hanbok that did nothing to conceal the lavishness of her breasts. As usual, Yoo-Min was acutely conscious of So-Yun's sumptuous breasts – they completely eclipsed her own meager wares. With an uncomfortable feeling, she thought, *How can I compete with those?* She hid her envy behind a mask of indifference and asked for green tea.

While she waited for her tea, she relaxed in her chair and took stock of her surroundings. An antique carved mahogany tilt-top table bearing a Yi Dynasty celadon bottle vase stood in a corner of the room. A nineteenth-century Korean wood-carved yin-yang phoenix hung on the wall to her right. An expensive handmade Chinese needlepoint rug covered the floor of the shop. She mentally noted that these were all items of considerable value.

While she admired these collectibles, So-Yun returned with her tea. Setting down a porcelain teapot on the black and gold lacquered table, So-Yun said, "This is a very soothing tea. It will calm you and open you up to new insights."

"Thank you."

"Would you like your fortune told?"

"Sure."

So-Yun sat down in a matching antique elm wood chair on the opposite side of the table and poured her a cup of tea. Then, reaching for her hand, So-Yun said, "Let's see what your future has in store for you."

Yoo-Min held out her hand. So-Yun took it up in her own. So-Yun's hands were as pallid as the white petioles of bok choy.

"What is the question you wish to have answered?" So-Yun asked, her breath faintly smelling of kimchi. "The question that is burning deep inside you now. The question that brought you to me."

Yoo-Min sensed that So-Yun was earnest about telling her fortune. With eyes bright as lanterns, she leaned forward and asked, "Will I find true love and happiness?"

"You have much anguish over this question."

"I do."

So-Yun examined her palm intently. After a moment of study, she said, "You ask this question with a particular person in mind."

"Yes."

So-Yun gazed steadfastly at her hand. Pressing firmly upon her mound of Venus at the base of her thumb, So-Yun said, "But there is another who haunts your thoughts."

Yoo-Min had a sinking feeling. She shifted restlessly in her chair. "What are you talking about?"

Tracing a line in Yoo-Min's palm with her finger, So-Yun said, "The one you seek, you will know him by his mark."

Yoo-Min tugged self-consciously at her skirt as So-Yun's wandering eyes rested on her legs. She thought achingly, *I need a hero. I need a hero to come and save me.*

"Would you like a cigarette?" asked So-Yun, letting go of her hand.

"I don't smoke."

"Yes, of course. I forgot. Do you mind if I do?"

"No. Of course not."

So-Yun reached for a pack of cigarettes and lit one up with a stainless steel lighter. She tossed the lighter on the table and took a puff. Her eyes turned to mere slits as she inhaled deeply. Satisfied, she set the cigarette in an ashtray and, leaning back in her chair, clasped her hands over a knee.

Yoo-Min stared at her feet. Her polished black shoes appeared elegant against the finely woven Chinese rug. She felt vaguely unsettled by what So-Yun had told her. She wanted to be left alone so she could think about things. Assuming a pose of utter boredom, her eyes drifted languidly around the room. They eventually rested on the carving of the yin-yang phoenix.

69

"Do you know the meaning of the yin-yang symbol?" asked So-Yun, noticing the direction of her gaze.

Hiding her annoyance, Yoo-Min shook her head.

"There is a Taoist belief," said So-Yun, touching her fingertips together. As if reciting from one of the ancient texts, she spoke slowly and thoughtfully, "In the beginning, only eternal souls were created by the creator of all things. Each soul was then divided into two; out of these separate halves were fashioned the souls of all living things, both male and female. For each individual soul in the world, male or female, there can be one and only one soul who matches it and can perfectly unite with it."

"Soul mates," Yoo-Min said, turning to face her friend with sudden interest.

"You might say that. The yin and the yang represent the separate halves of the eternal soul."

"I see."

"The taiji is a symbol of oneness, of the perfect union of two eternal souls – the female soul, or yin taiji, and the male soul, or yang taiji."

"I see."

So-Yun leaned forward. "Of course, these are modern times. It would be unconscionable to believe that perfect mates must always be male and female. I mean, two men could be equally perfect for each other – or two women."

Silence fell between them. The atmosphere of the teashop became eerily charged.

Yoo-Min focused her gaze on the intricate patterns of the needlepoint rug beneath her feet. The complex forms they created seemed to emulate the inscrutable repetition and symmetry of time and space. She felt a rush of elation as a marvelous thought occurred to her:

Is it possible that Suk-Jun and I are really one soul torn in two?

70

"But what happens," Yoo-Min asked, her almond eyes shining with fine mist, "when a soul meets its perfect match? Do they always recognize each other? Or is it possible that two souls who are a perfect match in the eternal sense may encounter each other in the flesh but fail to unite as one in perfect love?"

"Unfortunately, this is true," said So-Yun, nodding her head. She held Yoo-Min's eyes with her own. "Confined by the flesh, their apprehension of each other may be imperfect, and a rare opportunity is missed. Then, too, it may happen that one soul finds itself in the body of an animal, while the other soul is in the body of a man or a woman. Until the evolution of each brings them to the same level, they cannot be reunited. Their cycle of lives continues; only once every thousand years or so will these two perfectly matched souls encounter each other again. For these two souls, there is no liberation from this cycle until their union is complete."

Yoo-Min sat silently musing upon the possibilities. She knew without a doubt that she and Suk-Jun were perfectly matched. From the moment she had first set eyes upon him, she had sensed that they were destined to be with one another. They were soul mates; there could be no other explanation.

But what if they let this opportunity slip by? This possibility sobered her spirits immediately. She agonized over the thought: *Why, I would have to wait another thousand years or so before we met again!*

With her cigarette dangling from the side of her mouth, So-Yun excused herself from the table. She returned a moment later with a fine crystal European decanter and two

71

small glasses. Yoo-Min saw a strange root with long tendrils suspended in a golden liquid.

"It resembles a human body," she said quietly, transfixed by the sight. "Is it ginseng root?"

"Yes," So-Yun said, stabbing her cigarette into the ashtray. She held the decanter up to the light. "Panax ginseng. It's obvious from the human shape of the head and main root. Chinese ginseng is more carrot-shaped. This one's been cultivated for six years. You can tell the quality by the balance between the rhizome head and the main and lateral roots." She filled the glasses and handed one to Yoo-Min. "This is no ordinary ginseng. This one has special properties."

"What might those be?"

Yoo-Min watched as So-Yun held her glass in front of her face and turned it meditatively in her hands.

"It will help you remember."

"Remember what?"

"What you've forgotten."

So-Yun put the glass to her lips. "Geonbei," she said, draining its contents.

"Geonbei."

Yoo-Min drank from the glass. The ginseng tonic was surprisingly cool going down her throat. But when it reached her stomach she instantly felt a pleasing warmth working its way through her glandular system. Her organs pulsated with vigor and her skin seemed wonderfully alive and aware. She felt herself losing herself in the sensations of her body.

"You're very beautiful," she heard So-Yun speak in a voice dripping with desire.

"It's my nature," she heard herself say as the potion manipulated her senses.

"Yes, I can see that."

Through a smoky haze, she saw So-Yun flash china-white teeth at her. Her friend rose slowly from her chair like one of the mountains rising above the western plain. Walking around the low black and gold lacquered table, So-Yun stood majestically in front of her and peered down into her face.

"You have a rare beauty," So-Yun said to her, lifting her chin. So-Yun's eyes shone like ancient jade. "Beauty like yours appears only once a century or so."

Yoo-Min dimly thought, *Those words.* There was a ring of familiarity to those words. Was it something Suk-Jun had said to her? Or was it just another pick-up line she had heard a dozen times before?

So-Yun lowered her face close to hers. The scent of masculinized femininity filled her nostrils. Her head swam in a sea of sundry sensations. She faintly thought, *What is happening to me?* She said nothing when So-Yun's hand reached down and gently stroked her hair.

Like a flower gently collapsing its petals, she softly lowered the lids of her eyes.

So-Yun's breath washed warmly over her neck, inflaming her thoughts with strange passions. So-Yun's lips were close to her ears, whispering their praise:

"Never in my life have I beheld such immaculate beauty. You are the embodiment of perfection, my darling Yoo-Min."

Yoo-Min heard herself ask, "Do you find me beautiful?"

So-Yun's fingertips touched her face. "Yes."

"Do you burn for my beauty?"

So-Yun's palm caressed her cheek. "Yes."

"Would you die for my beauty?"

So-Yun's lips touched her neck. "Yes."

73

Yoo-Min had never known such sensations before – sensations of formless unity dissolving into ecstasy. She felt herself drifting out of her body. She seemed to be in a place far away, the veil of time removed from her face . . .

Her eyes flew open. Where was she? She saw herself as a young woman. Her name was Jung-Sin and she lived beneath the slope of a large mountain covered with tall pine trees. Mount Ong. The air was full of the songs of birds that lived in the forest. The sound of a rushing stream spread out in all directions as the water twisted and turned among the trees and rocks. On the slope of the mountain, compressed between the heavens and the earth, was a wooden temple. Happiness was abundant in her life. The good earth, the skies, the birds and the trees – she was thankful for these simple things.

Then, too, there was Han-Yong, the boy who loved her. Her heart gladdened with the thought of him. But Han-Yong was now an acolyte at the temple. As she in her vanity had rejected him, he in his pain had rejected the world.

A succession of images and sensations followed. She was walking barefooted among the trees along a serpentine path leading to the temple. The air was redolent with pine and patches of blue sky were sometimes visible through the branches. Eventually the trees thinned and the path opened up to a clearing. The temple loomed before her.

Sitting cross-legged under the blazing sun, at the summit of the temple steps, was an old monk. His shaved head was bent slightly forward and his eyes were closed in meditation. She recognized him immediately: Master Kwallŭk, the chief monk of the temple. The sight of this worthy figure distancing himself from the perturbations of the world humbled her.

74

She quietly approached the temple. The ancient one opened his eyes as if he had awoken from a deep sleep and blinked at her wonderingly. Suddenly his eyes were ablaze; she could feel the pull of her beauty on him. Eight were the liberations of Buddha, of which assurance and purpose through the appreciation of beauty was one. Hers was a pellucid beauty imitating the perfect beauty of the absolute – a beauty rarely glimpsed by ordinary men. Certainly this monk saw salvation in her. Yet it was salvation of a different sort; she was confident enlightenment would never be his. She rejoiced knowing that her beauty could sway not only men, but even monks – and if monks, then why not buddhas? She was deeply pleased.

With eyes flashing, she laughed and taunted him. "You're not a man," she said. "You're less than a man."

The monk sat untroubled by her rebuke. The darkness in his eyes was foreboding. Jung-Sin knew at once that her words, like pebbles cast into a pond, would create ripples that would spread through time, binding her in future lives to this monk against her will – such were the law of karma and the teachings of Buddha. She regretted her words.

She thought of Han-Yong. If only he would forgive her. Han-Yong was accomplished in the ten wholesome deeds. His love would save her.

Resolved, she went to search for him. By chance, she found him alone on the path to the temple, under the light of the moon, on the slope of the mountain. He was reciting the four noble truths and the twelvefold chain of dependent origination. His words were intermittently lost in the sounds of the cascading waters of a nearby spring.

"Han-Yong!"

He was clearly surprised to see her. His face beamed with unexpected pleasure.

75

"Jung-Sin!"

"I heard that you had become a monk," she said, stopping short in her approach.

"Yes, it's true."

"It's a noble calling," she said, unsure of herself.

"All callings are noble. All paths lead to the same destination."

"Do they treat you well?" she asked, desperate to make small talk.

"Yes. We work and we meditate. There is little time for anything else."

"It sounds so disciplined."

"It is."

A silence fell upon them. She wasn't sure whether Han-Yong was practicing a silent meditation. He seemed so different. He stood before her as one who was more heavenly than human.

"Your eyes," she said softly, struck by the light in them. His eyes shone more with the fire of earthly longing than divine inspiration.

"Yes?"

"The way you look at me."

"How is that?" he asked politely. His very being seemed to emanate the calmness that comes through virtuous conduct. But she knew differently.

"As if I'm the only woman in the world for you. As if there could never be anyone else."

Jung-Sin felt her breath cease as Han-Yong blushed the color of cherry blossoms. She was acutely cognizant of a sudden hush in the forest, as if the forest itself were waiting for the next words to be spoken between them.

"Do you still love me?" she asked softly, searching his face for the answer before he could speak.

"I am a monk now," Han-Yong said after a considered moment. There was a measure of pride in his voice. But it was false pride and she knew it.

"Yes. But you are a man, too."

"I loved you once," he said, lowering his lashes.

"And now?" she asked, raising her eyebrows.

"I cannot love you."

"Cannot? Or *will* not?"

"Does it matter?"

Jung-Sin's blood roiled and her eyes burst into fireballs. She loathed Han-Yong's sense of superiority. His nature was bright like the sun while hers was dark like the moon. They were a pair ordained by nature and yet they were so different. Hers was the lesser light and this infuriated her.

She demurely lowered her lashes. "Do you not find me beautiful?"

"I do."

"Do you not yearn for my beauty?

"I do." His breath was soft upon her face. "I have never laid eyes upon anyone as beautiful as you."

She edged closer, but not so close as to touch him. She could feel the warmth of his breath on her cheek. She gazed up into his eyes and asked: "Is it true what they say? That as a monk it is forbidden to touch a woman?"

"It's true," he said, nodding solemnly.

"You will never know a woman, then? As a man should know a woman?"

"No."

"Do you not yearn for the touch of a woman? Do you not desire to touch me?"

"I – I have no such desire."

"You deceive yourself, Han-Yong. I can see it in your eyes, see it in the way you still look at me." Jung-Sin's emotions seethed with suppressed rage. Softening her tone, she said, "A woman needs a man. She needs to feel a man, to be touched by him, to know him as surely as she knows her own breath."

Each word expressed her most fervent desire; each word rang with her sincerest convictions.

"Touch me, Han-Yong."

"Please, Jung-Sin," he softly pleaded, casting his eyes downward.

"Touch me," she insisted. She took his hand and laid it upon her breast. She could feel it trembling – or was it the quickening of her heart? She gazed into his eyes that were filled with impossible yearning, and cried: "Know what a woman truly feels like! Is this the filth you fear? Or is this the happiness you seek!"

Han-Yong did not move his hand from her breast. He let it linger there. Jung-Sin could sense the turmoil of his emotions as he debated whether the supple breast beneath his fingers was more real to him than the abstract reality to which he aspired. She could almost feel her victory; it was palpable, like a changing wind.

"I don't care what you think," she said, resting her head on his shoulder. Her hair was aflame in the silver moonlight. "Meditate and practice all you want. You'll never attain the six perfections. You'll never become a bodhisattva. You love me still and you'll love me always!"

The lush mountain scenery of ancient Paekche faded in Yoo-Min's consciousness, replaced by the modern decor of the teashop.

"What are you doing?" she mumbled, struggling to regain her awareness. The potent spell cast by the tonic dissipated.

So-Yun was on her knees, face twisted with ardor. Her ramie hanbok had come undone in front. The ribbons of the otgoreum hung loosely down. Her jade king melon breasts protruded like huge, overripe fruit. Her hands grasped frantically at Yoo-Min's breasts.

"Such beauty," So-Yun murmured in her ear, "I must have it."

"Are you crazy? Get away from me, So-Yun! Don't touch me!"

"Don't you see, Yoo-Min? We are one soul in two bodies. We are destined to be united!"

"I don't know what you're talking about! I'm not the one for you!"

"You *must* be the one! I *know* you are the one!"

"I am not! I swear it! I'm not the one you want!" Yoo-Min beat furiously at So-Yun's jade king melon breasts with her fists. Pushing So-Yun away, she bolted from her chair and swept up her bags. As forceful as a raging typhoon, she shoved her way past her friend and made for the door.

"Wait!" called So-Yun, rapping on the table three times in quick succession with her knuckles. "You forgot to pay!"

Yoo-Min paid her no attention. She shoved the door open and stepped into the street. Immediately she was hit by a blast of hot furnace air. As she rushed toward Myeong-dong station, the street scene wavered before her eyes – the sun was melting everything in sight.

"**K**wang-Chul, quit dreaming!"

Earlier that same day Kwang-Chul took refuge in Glade from the unbearable heat outdoors. Several businessmen gathered inside for a bite to eat and a midday libation. Glade opened its doors just before noon for the lunch crowd.

Behind the bar, nestled high in a corner, a flat screen plasma television set played highlights of a recent ssirum match between the current title-holder in the Paektu class and an upstart challenger.

Lost in thought, Kwang-Chul sat idly at the brushed steel bar and drummed upon its surface with his fingertips. Why had he not been able to consummate his desire for Yoo-Min in his dream? Was it just dumb chance that had prevented him from doing so – his inopportunely waking up just as he was about to do so? Or was it because he could not bring himself to despoil this impossible flower?

His mother's voice broke through his thoughts with the ferocity of a typhoon.

"Wake up! Don't be such a shiftless good-for-nothing all the time!"

He glanced up and saw his mother hovering over him. She looked positively fetching in a classic black slit ankle length dress with a high collar and bare shoulders. She lit up a cigarette and blew smoke in his face. Her eyes glared at him with a look that said: *Well, what are you waiting for?*

"Ai-goo!"

A groan went up from the patrons in Glade. The ssirum champion, wearing a blue sapta, had just thrown the challenger, wearing a red sapta, to the ground. Glade's patrons were apparently in favor of the underdog.

80

Kyung-A swung around to see what all the fuss was about. Kwang-Chul had no interest in the wrestling sport, notwithstanding the fact that it had been around since the time of the Three Kingdoms.

Withdrawing an ivory white business card from his shirt pocket, he studied it thoughtfully. The name and address of a teashop in Myeong-dong were embossed in handsome gold hangul on its surface. Underneath was the legend: *Fine Teas, Herbs & Collectibles.*

Yoo-Min had left the card on the table where she sat with Suk-Jun the night before. He had found it and wondered whether she had unconsciously left it on purpose. He couldn't help but feel that he was intended to find it. The forces of fate moved in mysterious ways. He believed that:

Behind the randomness and chaos of life there's unmistakable order. Seeming coincidences, distant and unrelated events, and apparently meaningless occurrences are all connected at some fundamental level.

Scrambling from his seat, he beat a path to the door and plunged into the inferno outdoors.

It felt like the sun was six inches from his head.

Making his way to the train station, he caught the train for Myeong-dong. The train ride was unbearable. There were no empty seats available and he was forced to stand in discomfort. Not only that, but the journey was overwhelming to his senses. The car was packed with a plethora of teenaged girls who surrounded him on all sides like a swarm of wiggling coccidia. Their young, shapely breasts heaved from the indefatigable summer heat. Perspiration coated their silken, ivory necks with a pale, slippery sheen. Their dazzling white bodies exuded a haughty sensuality while the scent of their powdered flesh, a tantalizing mixture of perfume and sweat, made every joint of his body ache with longing for such immaculate lotuses.

He was particularly absorbed with the sight of one bespectacled young girl who sat with her head down, strands of long black hair swirling across her face in some fantastic, undecipherable calligraphy, and her knees firmly pressed together so as not afford anyone the least glimpse of the pale white areas hidden beneath her ruffled skirt. This picture of refined modesty only inflamed his imagination to such a state that he found himself suddenly short of breath and feeling pangs of angina. He prayed that the train would soon reach its stop.

The train rolled into Myeong-dong. Kwang-Chul sauntered through the streets cognizant of an acute body hunger gnawing at him. He walked down one side street and then another, finding himself in a labyrinth of intriguing shops, exotic restaurants and rice-cake cafés serving steamed, boiled, and pounded ddeok. He spied the teashop in question. Entering, he heard the feeble tintinnabulation of a bell as the door closed behind him.

Behind a counter at the back of the teashop, a girl with shoulder length hair and squid ink eyes sat on a high stool. She was wearing a summer ramie hanbok that was undone in the front. The long ribbons of her otgoreum were untied and loosely hanging. Her thick, glossy black hair was tousled. A jade hairpin lay on the counter. Her temples glistened with drops of pearly sweat.

Overhead, a bamboo-bladed ceiling fan spun quietly, vainly trying to transmute the still, lifeless air into a nice cool breeze.

The teashop girl was eating japchae out of a green-glazed stoneware bowl with a pair of wooden chopsticks. Seeing him approach, she awkwardly tugged at her ramie hanbok and quickly tied the otgoreum to conceal her breasts. Satisfied that nothing could be seen, she gazed irritatingly at him and asked, "May I help you?"

Kwang-Chul saw from a gold-plated tag pinned to her hanbok that her name was Miss Kim. He said the first thing that came to his mind. "I'd like to buy some herbs."

"Sure."

"Pogolchi and Taeksa," he said, recalling the names of two herbs his mother used. By way of explanation, he added, "I have a yin deficiency in my kidneys."

"Hah! Those are for women! Pogolchi is used to strengthen the yang energy. If you have a yin deficiency, this will only complicate your condition. And you should not use Pogolchi if you are constipated."

"Constipated?"

"Pogolchi is used for treating chronic diarrhea."

Flushed with embarrassment, Kwang-Chul decided to keep his mouth shut. He took the opportunity to scrutinize a soapstone sculpture of Buddha in a corner of the room. He assumed that it was a replica. He had seen real ones just like it in the National Museum.

"A Maitreya Buddha from the Three Kingdoms," said Miss Kim, wrapping the glass noodles around her chopsticks.

Kwang-Chul stepped back for a better view and allowed the sculpture to sink fully into his consciousness. The Maitreya was seated. Its full, round face was smiling, giving the impression of one who has attained peace through understanding. A small usnisa protruded from the top of its head, signifying the Buddha's princely heritage and symbolizing his supreme wisdom and enlightenment. Kwang-Chul had seen other Maitreyas with large mandalas haloing the head; this one had none of that. He noticed that the earlobes had elongated perforations, suggesting the custom of wearing large gold earrings. The neck was thin and delicate and dissolved into gently sloping shoulders. The upper torso was modestly draped, while a jade pi disc hung from a simple belt. All in all, the gracefulness and sensuousness of the figure gave the unmistakable impression of a young girl.

Miss Kim came over and stood next to him. In a voice lowered in respect for this object of veneration, she discoursed softly:

"This Maitreya is from ancient Paekche. The naturalness and sensuousness of the figure leave no doubt. The face is more benevolent than Buddhas from Koguryŏ, the modeling more realistic than those from Silla. The Buddha's smile is characteristic of Paekche sculpture – it's often called the 'Paekche smile.'" Pointing to the pi disc, she said, "See the carvings of the characters for a dragon, tiger, and turtle? Those symbolize nature, while the disc itself, circular and thus infinite, symbolizes the universe. The simplicity of the pi disc, both in its shape and its decorations, convey a sense of harmony between the universe and its creations."

Awed by the Maitreya's sensual beauty and power, Kwang-Chul murmured, "It's beautiful." His sentiment stemmed not so much from the speech he had just heard as it did from the realization that this Maitreya was familiar to him in a manner he could not quite fathom. He yearned to touch the Maitreya, to caress its curves and feel its texture, but he refrained from doing so, primarily out of fear that the sculpture looked dangerously fragile but also out of respect for its religious significance. In any event, he couldn't imagine what price he would have to pay were he to damage it. He had the uneasy feeling that this was no ordinary

Maitreya; he was no longer sure whether it was even a replica.

"It's from the time of King Mu," remarked Miss Kim with an air of one knowledgeable in antiquities.

Kwang-Chul wasn't sure whether she was pulling his leg. King Mu had been the thirtieth king of ancient Paekche. It was said that one day King Mu and his wife saw three Maitreyas appear over the spot where the ruins of Mireuska were now located. The queen asked the king to build a temple in that spot.

"King Mu was famous for the many beautiful pavilions and gardens that he brought to Paekche," said Miss Kim dreamily. "He built Pangjang."

Kwang-Chul recalled bits and pieces of the legend. In honor of the great Taoists and perhaps with some hope of attaining immortality himself, King Mu had a lake dug to the south of the palace and surrounded it with wispy willow trees. In the center of this lake, he had an island built and named it 'Pangjang.' Anapchi in Kyŏngju was fabled for its beauty with its mountain islands and flowering plants and rare birds and animals, but it was said that Pangjang was far superior in every respect.

Miss Kim sat down on her stool and reached for her chopsticks. Picking up a clump of glass noodles, she said:

"Not so many years later the kingdom was conquered by Silla troops."

Outside, a busload of passengers supporting the reunification of the two Koreas passed by with bullhorns blaring. Glancing out the window, Kwang-Chul said, "Yes, when Silla joined forces with T'ang China. General Kyebaek lead his death bands against the great Silla general, Kim Yusin. He was defeated at the battle of Hwangsanbul."

"Yes, I remember that," murmured Miss Kim, her mouth full of glass noodles. "The cliff –" She left the sentence unfinished.

Kwang-Chul gazed at her thoughtfully. When Silla invaded Paekche, three thousand court ladies of Paekche had thrown themselves off a nearby cliff into the Paekma River rather than submit themselves to be raped by the marauding army. It was said that their colorful hanboks resembled billowing flowers as they fell. This story always evoked strong emotions in him. He supposed it was the ineffable beauty of their actions. "I guess you mean Nakhwaam Cliff," he said.

She lowered her eyes, but not before he had seen the tears welling in them. "They were pushed," she said softly, turning her head towards the window.

He stared at her curiously. "Do you mean the court ladies?" A fantastic notion came to him. But before he gave it voice, he halted, feeling a trifle foolish. Bowing his head, he thought, *No, that's impossible.*

Miss Kim gazed absentmindedly into space as if she hadn't heard him. Then, wiping her eyes with the sleeve of her hanbok, she said, "I'll make some tea."

Before Kwang-Chul could make up his mind whether to accept her offer, she added:

"It will restore the balance in your kidneys."

K wang-Chul took a seat at one of the black and gold lacquered tables by the window of the shop. Feeling dispirited, he tried to empty the vessel of his mind, but his thoughts were too agitated to obey.

Through his lashes, he watched as Miss Kim pulled out an electric hot plate and set it on the table and plugged it into a wall socket. As the dull charcoal coils of the hot plate began to glow a dirty red, she poured spring water from a plastic bottle into a copper kettle and placed the kettle on the hot plate. Opening an airtight canister of tea, she savored the aroma and offered him a whiff. The smell of young tea leaves tweaked his nostrils.

"Teas," said Miss Kim, "are classified according to several methods. The most common method for green teas is according to the time of the season the leaves are plucked. Woojeon tea leaves are picked in the first blush of spring before the day known as Koku, which comes in mid-April. Woojeon tea will give you clarity of mind and quietude of spirit. Sejak tea is gathered between Koku and Ipha, which is in the beginning of May. It'll refresh your organs and restore your body to health. Jungjak tea is gathered after Ipha and is best for stimulating conversation.

"Woojeon tea," continued Miss Kim, "is the finest grade of green tea in Korea. Only the fresh tips of the leaves are used. If the leaf is fully-developed, it's considered too coarse to produce the exquisitely intense flavor that commands the highest price in tea rooms."

While the water heated, Miss Kim prepared a tea set consisting of a teapot, two ceramic cups and wooden saucers, a small lipped bowl for pouring, a larger bowl for the discarded water used to warm the cups, a ceramic saucer for the lid of the teapot, and a bamboo spoon. After a moment, Kwang-Chul heard her humming to herself.

"In the old days," she explained to him, "the kettle would hang from a tripod over a charcoal-filled brazier. Water heated in this manner would sing over the fire." She put a finger to her lips. "Listen." She cocked her head. "Do you hear it?"

Kwang-Chul didn't hear a thing, but wishing to be polite he nodded as if he had.

"Yes. I do."

"The water is at full boil," Miss Kim announced perfunctorily, turning down the rheostat on the hot plate.

Kwang-Chul knew that the secret of preparing Woojeon tea was to cool the water down to at least fifty degrees Celsius. He surmised that Miss Kim had been schooled in the art of preparing and serving tea, for she did so skillfully. He nodded with approval as she poured hot water into the small lipped bowl. From there she poured the water into the empty teapot to warm the pot. From the teapot she poured it into an empty cup, and from the cup into the large bowl. Then she poured more water into the lipped bowl, and while it cooled she put a scoopful of tea into the teapot.

Kwang-Chul was mesmerized by her mastery. He observed that she knew precisely when the water in the small lipped bowl had cooled sufficiently. She poured it gently from the bowl into the teapot, just enough for one cup. Silently measuring the time, she allowed the tea to steep for three minutes, the proper amount of time to bring out the full flavor of the tea without making the taste too strong or bitter. While the tea steeped, she poured a new measure of hot water into the lipped bowl to prepare it for a second serving.

She poured the first serving into his cup. She placed the cup on a saucer and placed the saucer in front of him. The etiquette of serving tea did not permit her to pass the cup from hand to hand. She said:

"Properly brewed, the color of this Woojeon tea should not be so dark as to be opaque nor so clear as to be transparent. It must be wonderfully translucent like the jade green waters of a reed pond bathed in summer's light."

Kwang-Chul scrutinized the contents of the cup. The color of the tea was like the hue of a limpid pool of blades of grass and beautiful green buds. He heard Miss Kim intone:

"The fragrance must be neither so strong as to be coarse and offensive nor so weak as to be imperceptible; rather, it must be tantalizingly subtle and call to mind the scent of mountain dew on a clear summer night."

He inhaled deeply to savor the tea's fragrance. He knew at once that she had achieved the proper proportion of tea to water and had steeped it just right. As he nodded, Miss Kim softly said:

"The tea should taste rich but at the same time delicate. It should invoke a sense of purity and the promise of perfection."

He lightly sipped the tea and allowed its taste to linger on his tongue. A cleansing sensation awakened in him. He took a deeper sip and allowed the tea to warm his throat. Instantly he felt his heart and mind clear. Stillness flowed through him.

"Ah," he said, brimming with appreciation. He set the cup down and leaned back and cradled his knees.

"Drinking tea is a spiritual practice," said Miss Kim airily. "Knowing how to drink tea is to understand Sŏn. To drink tea, one empties the cup. To understand Sŏn, one empties oneself. It's written that the man who has a true understanding of how to drink tea will find that in the taste of tea there is contained the truth of all the ten thousand forms of the universe." She picked up the bamboo spoon and pointed to an indentation in the middle of it. "This signifies the one true mind to which the ten thousand forms of the universe return. The bamboo spoon should be six *chi*. The six *chi* represent – "

"The six perfections," Kwang-Chul said, suddenly perking up

"What do you know of the six perfections?" asked Miss Kim, her eyes narrowing suspiciously.

"To know the six perfections is to be a bodhisattva."

Miss Kim studied him with a considered look. "And do you think *you* can become a bodhisattva?"

"Day and night I've struggled against what is human in me to reach what is divine in all," he said.

"The desire of the spirit and the desire of the flesh are one and the same," she said coolly. "Spirit and flesh are delusions; to be human is to be deluded."

"I've worked very hard to purge myself of all desire," said Kwang-Chul dryly. He hadn't expected the purity of his motives and the power of his intentions to be challenged. With a sigh, he added, "All my life I've practiced the five abstentions and the ten wholesome deeds."

He offered his cup for a refill. Miss Kim filled it a second time and said, "No doubt you have. But know that the five abstentions and ten wholesome deeds are but the very beginning of training. Even an ordinary person can undertake them, for they require no skill but only abstinence and willingness. But to understand the four noble truths, to transcend the twelvefold chain of dependent origination, to attain the six perfections – these are not the undertakings of humans or even heavenly beings. They belong to the ranks of sravakas and pratyekabuddhas and bodhisattvas."

Kwang-Chul was surprised by the depth of her knowledge. He fidgeted as she fixed him with a meticulous gaze. For a moment he felt like a dubious specimen of insect being pinned by an entomologist for further study. He lowered his eyes and drank his tea to mask his unease.

Miss Kim paid him no mind. "*If* you succeed in controlling your emotions and extinguishing your sentience," she said, "you may in due course become acquainted with the three knowledges. You will gain knowledge of past lives, of the principle of karma, of the extinction of the outflows. But even then your understanding will be shallow and lacking uniformity. It will be like the burbling waters of a rippling brook, not deep and consonant like the still waters of the great oceans. In time, you may progress further and demonstrate evidence of the six supernatural powers."

"The power to see at a distance," said Kwang-Chul thoughtfully, recalling a treatise by Kihwa – one of the great meditation masters of the Chosŏn dynasty – he had once read. He added, "And the power to hear at a distance."

"The power to read minds," offered Miss Kim, pouring him another cup of tea. Protocol required no more than three servings from the same batch of tea.

"The power to know one's past lives and the past lives of others," he said, tingling with a burgeoning sense of excitement.

"Yes."

"The power to do anything at will."

"Yes."

"And the power to be anywhere at will," he said softly, gazing into his tea.

Miss Kim's eyes met his. She casually leaned back in her chair and asked him nonchalantly:

"Why did you come here?"

"I told you," he said, affecting calm but roiling but with emotion. "I came to buy herbs for my mother."

"I know what you said. What do you *really* want?"

Kwang-Chul sunk in his chair, weighted by the uncomfortable feeling that she knew precisely what was on his mind.

"You want her, don't you?"

"Eh?"

"Yoo-Min. She's amazing, isn't she?" said Miss Kim in an offhanded way. "The way she attracts men – or women, for that matter. It's impossible to resist her. No one can. Hers is a beauty to die for."

The door of the teashop slid open and the bell above it tinkled ceremoniously. A moment later Suk-Jun entered the teashop. Suk-Jun's green jade eyes fanned the room and lit upon Kwang-Chul. Kwang-Chul felt himself collapsing into a nullity.

Miss Kim frowned. Darkness filled her eyes as she added under her breath:

"Or kill for."

Yoo-Min spent the train ride home deep in the throes of self-wrought misery. Try as she might, she could not refrain from conceiving all sorts of strange notions. Her imagination was strong and active and this only intensified her feelings of uneasiness.

She pondered the meaning of her dream in the teashop. She wondered if it was a recollection of a previous life. It had been so vivid that she thought it might be.

She felt a profound sadness poking a hole in her heart. What kind of life did she have as the girl Jung-Sin? What had happened to her? How did she die? Her inability to answer these and other questions pressed upon her with a suffocating weightiness.

Her almond eyes brimmed with tears. She thought of all those souls who had once lived and loved and died. They were forever gone and forgotten. No one would ever know who Jung-Sin was, no one would ever care that long ago Jung-Sin had walked the green and tawny earth and breathed the pine-scented air of the forests, or that she had once been loved by a boy named Han-Yong. What had become of him? What did it matter? She herself would one day be dead. There was no preventing it; such was the fate of all. But the world would go inexorably on and others would come and go, and after enough time and generations had passed, no one would know or even care that she had ever lived, much less loved.

Unable to control the welling of her emotions, she began to sob; the cruelty and senselessness of life was unfathomable. What was the point of living if only to die? She wanted to live and to keep on living, to live and love without cessation. But one day she would be dead and that would be the end of it. The realization that her life was so ephemeral struck her deeply.

Arriving home, she prepared a tepid bath with salts to wash away the sweat and the smells of the city. Undressing, she slipped into the tub and felt the water's cool warmth seep into her skin. As the tension that tied her muscles into knots dissipated, her thoughts drifted to the teashop and her memories of Jung-Sin, if they really were memories. In the teashop, where So-Yun's collection of curios and historical artifacts nurtured fanciful thoughts, even the impossible seemed real. But with enough time having passed to dull the imagination, and surrounded by the familiar objects in her apartment, she was less sure of things. Even So-Yun's unwanted affection seemed trifling.

Her head swam in a sea of sultry sensations. Threads from her past dangled in her mind; she seized upon one and followed it. It took her through the hollow years of her adolescence and the tattered ruins of her childhood; through hazy, wispy traces of her infancy; through phantoms of the past too indistinct to discern; and further still, to the slope of the mountain where she once lived long, long ago.

Indistinct images of a temple rose in her consciousness; she instinctively felt it to be an evil place. Wisps of incense rose languidly in the air; in the cloud-like reality before her, she beheld vague, fantastic shapes – great, gilded buddhas with sightless eyes; robeless monks flogging each other with thorny branches and achieving paroxysms of ecstasy; beautiful, naked young boys with lotus-white faces in the embraces of bony old men with purple-headed jajis taut as bows. She saw in the turbulent atmosphere of her thoughts their supple, naked bodies merging together, limbs contorting and twisting, flesh fusing with flesh, and her blood turned colder than the waters of the river Tae. Above everything loomed a horrific creature, its soft pink petals swimming in the pale light like the tentacles of a large sea anemone – Master Kwallŭk.

Everything she saw had a hallucinatory quality to it, as if she had been given a strange and powerful drug.

The bath water lapped at her lips. Through slit almond eyes she watched as Kwallŭk's head transformed itself into a colorful nylon mesh bath puff floating on the surface of the water.

"Ha, ha! I must be losing it," she said, relieved to know that it was just a trick of her mind, the lingering effects of the ginseng potion So-Yun had given her, she supposed.

She pushed the netted bath puff away with her foot. Keeping her foot out of the water, she took a moment to admire the symmetry of her perfectly-shaped toes. Her toes glowed ruddily from the warmth of the bath.

"They look like delicate rose petals," she said admiringly, feeling pleased with herself.

Lowering her foot into the water, she half-closed her eyes and swam in sensations of contentment. Her senses homed into the drone of the air conditioner in the next room. In no time at all she was lulled by the hypnotic effect of its steady hum.

Unfettered by concerns, her thoughts drifted upon a tranquil sea.

And then suddenly she was Jung-Sin again. She was in her home under the shadow of the mountain. Darkness covered her like a thick cloth. She felt the presence of the ancient one near to her and she trembled. How was this possible? Master Kwallŭk must be one who had attained the six supernatural powers, the fifth of which was the power to be anywhere at will.

Her body was drenched with sweat. The air was dank and had a smell of wanton indulgence – and fear. Was it the pleasures he gave her that she feared or the power that he had attained? He only came to her at night as she slept, and such that none could see him, not even she. Yet she felt his jaji thick as bamboo and just as stiff.

After the first night that the ancient one had come to her, she avoided the temple at all costs. But the old monk came in the night once more, and once more still. Where was Han-Yong? Why didn't he save her? She hadn't heard from him since the night she had found him under an opalescent moon on the forest path to the temple.

She didn't know what to do. Her mother, attuned to her emotions, sensed that something was amiss. One night as she lay on her bed of straw awaiting her unseen lover, she saw through the slits of her eyes her mother standing over her with what seemed to be a waterfall of slender, shimmering eels in her hands. When she realized the significance of the lustrous strands of pure silk her mother held, she wept in silence.

And then she was running through the mountain forest on a steamy summer night. Fish-silvery light from a hidden moon streamed like icicles through the treetops. Her steps were light but quick; there was urgency in them.

She reached a clearing in the forest. It was the same clearing where she had seen Han-Yong reciting the four noble truths and the twelvefold chain of dependent origination. The memory of that encounter tugged at her heart. She quickly strangled it. She looked up and saw that overhead storm clouds were rapidly gathering. The mountain air swelled with humidity, threatening to burst with the least provocation. Undoing her garments, she let them slip to the ground. Her naked body wavered in the night like a fantastic apparition. She lay on the forest floor on a blanket of fresh pine needles. The earth, the trees, the ominous skies above, all pulsed with an eerie rhythm, an ebb and flow mimicking the throbbing of her heart.

The clouds overhead split their seams. Rain slashed the skies and poured through the trees. She gazed at the black treetops, seeing nothing but an impenetrable darkness. Her eyes, feverish with single-minded purpose, filled with rain. Lifting her legs, she spread them apart and bent them at the knees. She tore at the flesh between her legs, digging and clawing with her fingernails, rending the silk threads that her mother had used to bind and protect her womanhood from the perils of the night. With her fingers she parted the raw softness between her legs, grimacing as the pressure between her legs increased until she could stand it no longer.

Lightning ripped the heavens asunder. She moaned loudly with chilling pain. Blood gushed from between her rain-drenched legs and soaked the forest floor. She told herself she mustn't be faint of heart. She felt the life flourishing inside her struggling to free itself from her womb. She nearly passed out as undulations of intense pain swept through her. The pain was excruciating beyond anything she had imagined. She was sure that she would lose her mind. She opened her mouth to scream but her fear of discovery was so great that all she could issue was a horrifically silent shriek. The blood between her legs kept flowing. She couldn't stem the tide. She felt weak and dizzy. With a deep, heart-wrenching sadness, she knew that she was going to die.

Yoo-Min came to her senses in a panic with the realization that she was drowning. Water was filling her lungs and she was choking – she must have fallen asleep in the tub. She scarcely knew what happened next; her instinct

97

to survive took over. She broke through the surface of the water and flung her head over the side of the tub and began gagging. Water streamed from her nose and throat; she couldn't breathe. Tears flooded her eyes at the thought that she might die.

And then the crisis was over. A rush of cool air found her lungs; her body trembled with relief. She hung onto the side of the tub and thanked her good fortune. But the thought that had plagued her for days darkened her mind:

Am I pregnant? But how?

Limp with exhaustion, Yoo-Min felt as if the very life had been sucked out of her. The thought that she might be pregnant worried and elated her at the same time.

Feeling edgy, she put on some music for ambience. She chose the piano version of a popular song about love and jealousy and betrayal, and set her music player so that it would play the song over and over.

Laying down on her yo, she closed her eyes and felt her feelings come alive as the music spoke to her soul. Love and jealousy and betrayal. The themes resounded in her brain like resonating tympani. She wondered about her putative life as Jung-Sin. Were her reminiscences of a life long ago nothing more than the burgeoning life within her manifesting itself as memories?

The afternoon passed and blended into evening. The crepuscular skies above Seoul turned dark.

The shadows on the wall grew long until they weren't shadows anymore.

The melancholic notes of the piano played upon her senses; she sunk into a morass of sadness. She thought about her ceaseless yearning to find love. One day she hoped to find true love. But for now, true love, the kind of love that would give meaning to her life, seemed as distant and forlorn as the forgotten love of Jung-Sin.

As the music continued unabated in the background, she slipped into a hypnagogic state.

She dimly felt someone close to her. Who was it? Unknown lips fiercely pressed upon hers. Hands shamelessly touched her flesh. Tongues of flame were licking at her breasts. She thought that she would go out of her mind. Before she knew it, the thing was done.

She woke up suddenly with her heart beating madly. The music was still playing. She bolted upright and peered deep into the shadows of the room.

"Who's there?" She studied first the door and then the window. "Is anyone there?"

She searched the room with her eyes. They lit upon a wall clock and she saw by its luminous background that she had dozed for almost an hour. Her sense of time was dilated. It seemed like she had napped for hours. The pounding of her heart wouldn't cease.

On an impulse, she picked up the phone and called So-Yun. The bonds of friendship were strong; it was as if nothing unusual had passed between them. She mentioned her queer feeling that someone had been in her room while she was sleeping.

"Maybe it was a ghost," she heard So-Yun say.

"Do you believe in ghosts?"

"Yes. Ch'eng Hao taught that ghosts and spirits are spiritual forces, one negative, one positive. And Sŏ Kyŏngdŏk said that men and ghosts are coagulations of material force, but of different strength and speed." She heard So-Yun pause, then ask, "Whose ghost do you suppose it might have been?"

"I don't know."

"Tell me what happened."

"Nothing. He just watched me."

"He just watched you?"

"Yes."

"He didn't touch you?"

She hesitated. Had something in her voice betrayed her?

"No," she lied, examining herself carefully. Feeling that things had become a little too personal, she ended the conversation abruptly.

Fighting to control her emotions, she rose from her yo. Unmindful of her nakedness, she slipped into the chair in front of her vanity. To kill her thoughts, she picked up a brush and gently stroked her hair, doing one side methodically and evenly, and then the other. When she finished combing her hair, she set down the brush and stretched out her legs. Her skin was firm and glistening. She touched her nipples. A tingling warmth flowed languidly through her body. She blushed. The redness in her cheeks spread quickly, like a rose abruptly opening its petals.

But the pleasant warmth she felt was supplanted by a creeping doubt. Curling her toes, she couldn't help wonder whether Suk-Jun really loved her. Was it love smoldering like coals in his eyes the night they had met or merely desire? In the dimness of the room, with the encroaching night breathing new life into her feelings of bleakness, she was no longer certain whether Suk-Jun loved her after all.

All the way back to Glade, Kwang-Chul kept brooding over the events of the day. To begin with, he couldn't make heads or tails of his conversation with Miss Kim in the teashop. Her emotionally charged, intuitive nature absolutely mystified him. She seemed to dwell on another plane of existence altogether.

And what in the world was Suk-Jun doing at the little teashop in Myeong-dong? That was an odd coincidence. He couldn't help feeling that there was more to their encounter than met the eye. Seeing Suk-Jun, he had felt the kind of enmity one felt towards a natural enemy.

When he exited the train in It'aewon-dong, a well-dressed, bearded foreigner sporting a black turban approached him and said in a thick accent, "I see that you are a holy man. Please, pray for me." Kwang-Chul didn't know what to say. He just nodded his head and without thinking blurted, "Sure, I'll pray for you." This seemed to satisfy the foreigner, who flashed a gold-toothed smile and shuffled away with a limping gait.

When he arrived back at Glade his mother was busy consoling the owner of the jindo that had been served up as boshintang to Yoo-Min and Suk-Jun. The poor little fellow looked as if he had lost his best friend in the whole world.

Kyung-A immediately marshaled him into the kitchen. "Where the hell have you been?" She jerked a thumb over her shoulder. "He came looking for his dog," she told him, her beady black eyes glaring at him accusingly. "Someone saw you bring it here."

"What did you say?"

"What do you think? I told him that you don't even like dogs. Why would you want his?"

101

"Did that satisfy him?"

His mother didn't bother to respond. She brusquely brushed him aside and made herself busy preparing a savory dish over the stove. Kwang-Chul suddenly had the feeling that she was up to no good.

"What are you doing?"

He poked his head over her shoulder and sniffed the air inquisitively, sneezing as a particularly pungent aroma wafted up his nostrils.

"Getting rid of the evidence," she replied. Her eyes were smoldering with satisfaction.

"What evidence?"

"What do you think, stupid?"

"What? Wait a minute! You don't mean you're giving him *boshintang?*"

"Sure! Why not? He has a lot of nerve coming in here like that and accusing you of stealing his jindo!"

"You can't feed him his own dog!"

"He'll never know!"

Later, he begrudgingly had to admit that his mother was a genius. After downing two bowls of boshintang, the jindo owner was in a gay mood. He apologized to them both and thanked Kyung-A especially for her hospitality. Fresh off her victory, his mother grinned at him triumphantly and called for shots of soju, but he was in no mood to celebrate.

The rest of the afternoon passed in a whirlwind of distraught emotions. Trudging up to his room, he threw himself on his bed and let his imagination torture him for the better part of an hour. He couldn't stop thinking about Yoo-Min. He recalled how she and Suk-Jun had cozied up to one another in Glade the night before. He painfully remembered how they kept casting shameless glances at each other over bowls of fresh, steaming boshintang while he stood helplessly by like a fat, limp noodle. Finally, he recalled with disgust how they had ventured into the diamond night like two long-tailed weasels intent on consummating their mutual lust.

After that, his imagination furiously spun its wheels. He envisioned Suk-Jun smoothly putting on a number of slick moves calculated to defeat Yoo-Min's most stalwart defenses – thrust and parry, thrust and parry – and her half-hearted resistance and all-too-willing surrender; their bodies colliding in the darkness like wild animals in fierce combat; the frenzied, blistering climax with Suk-Jun grunting and groaning like an insatiable sow, and Yoo-Min on her back, eyes slit like razor cuts as she lay impaled on a sacrificial altar of love, alternating between piercing screams of ecstasy and deep-throated sobs of pleasure; and then the inevitable dénouement, the sighs of mutual satisfaction and fatigue, the gentle uncoupling of their sweat-soaked bodies, and the feigned sleep as they lay on stained sheets with their naked backs to each other, savoring the indelible memory of the night's pleasure while refusing to acknowledge the emptiness gnawing inside each of them like parasitic worms.

It was simply too much for him. Wearied by the onslaught of images parading mercilessly across his mind, he fell into a light sleep. Visions of Yoo-Min danced in his dreams, but they were short-lived. The anxiety of not knowing what really had transpired between her and Suk-Jun, coupled with the frustration he felt from not being able to stoke her feelings for him, bubbled in his brain even while he dozed – he woke up.

Glade was already bustling with business when he went downstairs a short while later. Wearing a snazzy, single-breasted royal blue suit and pink dress shirt, with a complementary pink handkerchief emblazoned with blue polka dots stuffed in the handkerchief pocket, he hoped to cut a dashing enough figure so as to catch Yoo-Min's eye that evening when she reported for work – and maybe even capture her heart .

As usual, Chan-Woo was working behind the bar. Kyung-A sat cross-legged on a barstool watching the plasma screen television with her silk-pleated designer skirt hiked up her shapely thighs. She was munching on sannakji – pieces of live octopus seasoned with sesame oil and sprinkled with sesame seeds – served on a white porcelain dish. Kwang-Chul ambled over.

"What're you watching?"

"*Silk and Sŏn*! Sit here!" His mother patted the adjacent barstool. "This is the season finale." Her beetle-black eyes were luminous with appreciation. "There've been one hundred and fifty-five episodes so far and I've seen them all!"

Kwang-Chul was impressed with his mother's devotion. "What's it about?" Taking the offered seat, he picked up a pair of chopsticks and greedily snatched a couple of squiggling pieces of live octopus. His face turned sour as Suk-Jun appeared on the television screen flashing an enlightened smile. Suk-Jun looked almost transcendent in the long, flowing robes of a monk, the garb of his character.

"It's marvelous! It stars Park Suk-Jun. He also directs each segment and writes all the scripts," said Kyung-A, fluttering her thick lashes like a doting schoolgirl.

"Is there nothing he can't do?" asked Kwang-Chul, bristling with resentment.

"Don't be jealous," scolded Kyung-A, wagging her finger. She gazed admiringly at Suk-Jun's handsome face on the screen and sighed so heavily that her breasts were primed to burst out of her black, low cut blouse. "He's so dreamy!"

Kwang-Chul raised his eyebrows in disbelief. "Not you, too?" He cast a disdainful eye at the stunning image of Suk-Jun on television. "Where's his hair?"

"He's a monk," said Kyung-A dryly. "He's not supposed to have hair."

"Damn, he looks good even without hair!"

His mother gave him a brief synopsis. "The story takes place long ago. Park Suk-Jun plays a monk who must choose between the woman he loves and enlightenment."

"Sounds silly."

Kwang-Chul was reluctant to admit that the story piqued his interest. To demonstrate his indifference, he pulled out a stainless steel nail clipper from his pocket and began idly clipping his nails.

"You missed the first half of the program," chimed in Chan-Woo from across the bar. He winked at Kwang-Chul as if to say, *You haven't missed anything.*

Kwang-Chul forced a yawn to keep up pretenses. He turned his attention to the television screen. The picturesque scene of a green mountain beneath a cerulean sky faded to an interior shot of Suk-Jun kneeling before an old monk, whose shadow fell darkly upon the handsome young actor. Behind the old monk were gilt-bronzed images of the Buddha, while towering above them was an agalmatolite Maitreya seated upon a lotus-petaled pedestal, its face etched with an inscrutable smile. Kwang-Chul thought that it looked just like the one in the teashop.

The old monk gazed quizzically upon Suk-Jun.

"You would leave this temple of light and understanding and return to the world of darkness and ignorance? For what purpose?"

Suk-Jun bowed his shaven head until it was but a breath above the pinewood floor of the temple.

105

"I – I love."

"What did you say?"

"Master, I cannot eat, I cannot sleep, I cannot meditate! My meditations are not upon the great nothingness that we all seek, but upon her and her alone. I can think of nothing but her. If this is not love, what is it?"

Sighing deeply, Kyung-A put a hand over her heart and fluttered it.

"Oh, give me a break," groaned Kwang-Chul. "He's half your age."

"Precisely," said Kyung-A, smiling. Her moon-shaped face bounced up and down like a bobbing fishing float.

"It is desire," replied the ancient monk, caressing Suk-Jun's head affectionately. "You would be wise to remember that desire is the cause of transmigration. To free yourself from the never-ending cycle of birth and death and rebirth, you must overcome your desires. If you cannot overcome your desires, there is no possibility of true enlightenment, there is only endless transmigration. You will die and be born again, and die once more and be born once more, for generations upon generations."

"I have dreams, Master!" wailed Suk-Jun, pulling at the flesh of his head.

"What sort of dreams?" wondered Kwang-Chul under his breath.

"What sort of dreams?" asked the ancient one sullenly.

"Dreams of *her!*"

The ancient one's face darkened like a new moon. "Lust clouds your thoughts and obstructs your wisdom. It binds you to this mundane world as a human being."

"Who's he supposed to be, anyway?" asked Kwang-Chul, jerking a thumb at the old monk while he chewed thoughtfully on a squirming piece of live octopus.

His mother dug her long acrylic nails into his forearm. She cast him a brief glance, the color blanched from her face. Kwang-Chul thought that she looked like a wraith. She hoarsely whispered:

"Kwallŭk! The master of the temple!"

Kwang-Chul felt the air rush out of his lungs. Every student of Korean Buddhism knew that name. Kwallŭk! The noble monk from Paekche famous for bringing the teachings of Buddha to Japan, as well as books on astronomy, geography, and the occult. A master of tun-chia, the art of making oneself invisible. Was this Kwallŭk, the monk whose mind flower had shone upon ancient Paekche with the serene radiance of a true bodhisattva, the same Kwallŭk whom she was talking about?

"Hey! What's wrong with you?" His mother's face was etched with concern. "Are you alright?"

"It's nothing, nothing," he wheezed, choking on a piece of live octopus. Tears pooled in his eyes as he gripped the edge of the brushed steel bar top. His lips turned blue as he struggled for air.

"How many times have I told you?" admonished Kyung-A, pounding his back with her fist. "The suction cups will stick to your throat if you don't chew thoroughly!"

Managing to swallow the offending tentacle, Kwang-Chul wiped the tears from his eyes with his knuckles.

"Women are foul, full of filth, capable of corrupting a man with impure thoughts," snarled the ancient monk, his mouth scarcely more than a crack in a parched landscape. "A man must avoid them lest his thoughts become polluted and unclean and incapable of attaining purity."

"He must be a gelding," said Kyung-A disdainfully, jerking her thumb at the old monk. "You know. Snip-snip." She made a scissors motion with two fingers.

"Ouch, that hurts!" Kwang-Chul screwed his face in mock pain.

"Is it wrong for a man to deny his natural tendencies?" cried Suk-Jun. "Is not a man born for only one purpose: to love a woman?"

The ancient one's face transformed from one of paternalistic patience to one of strong curiosity. "Love? What can a monk know of love? Love is for humans, not for those who would be bodhisattvas!"

"Perhaps I was not meant to be a monk," said Suk-Jun, his face mantled with shame. "Night and day I have meditated to penetrate the dharma and attain the Lotus Paradise, but all I can think of is her!"

"Who is this one who darkens your sight?"

"She lives in the village under the shadow of the mountain, Master. Her name is Jung-Sin."

"Jung-Sin," repeated the ancient one reverently, as if chanting one of the sacred mantras. "Jung-Sin."

"Master, you seem to know her!"

The ancient one bowed his head.

"I have heard of her."

"Master, is it possible?"

"When a fresh wind blows, the clouds part. When the clouds part, light shines everywhere. Her beauty is unsurpassed."

"Indeed, Master, her beauty would brighten the universe."

"But she is beautiful to a fault, young monk, and sought after by many. It is rumored that her beauty would even entice a bodhisattva." The ancient monk's eyes were smoldering like forest embers. "If a bodhisattva can be tempted by such beauty, how can a mere monk such as you resist such a temptress?"

"She is not a temptress, Master!"

"She is a woman!"

Suk-Jun's jaw dropped. His eyes widened with sudden illumination.

"And you are a monk!"

"What of it?" The ancient one glowered. "As monks we renounce the world and commit ourselves to lives of deprivation and meditation. We endeavor day and night to overcome ignorance, sensation, desire, attachment, and even birth and death, because we seek to realize the one true nature. But there is more than one path to enlightenment, and we need seek our nirvana where we find it." He raised his eyes upwards, as if contemplating a high, unreachable realm. "Beauty such as hers is not of this world; it belongs to another sphere altogether. In Jung-Sin's transcendent beauty, I've seen intimations of the divine!"

"She is a woman to be loved, Master, not a perfection to be attained! You can no more possess her beauty than you can seize the air!"

"She is with child," the ancient one sneered.

"No!"

The ancient one's eyes glazed with rapture. "The essence of what is human in me has commingled with the essence of what is sublime in her. Would you not suppose that such a commingling will bring me closer to the one true nature, not only in the present but for generations to come?"

Eyes blazing with vengeance, Suk-Jun leapt to his feet. "If one evil goes unpunished, a thousand more will appear!"

The ancient one stood unwavering, eyes shod with blood. Waving a desiccated hand, he summoned a pair of snarling, large-headed brindled mastiffs out of the murkiness.

"Ugh," said Kwang-Chul disgustingly, turning his head away and burying it in his mother's shoulder. "Dogs."

"There, there," said Kyung-A, patting his head affectionately.

The sonorous background music, which had been inexorably building up, rose to a crescendo of thundering drums and clashing cymbals. Kwang-Chul raised his head in time to see the enraged beasts hurl themselves upon the young monk. The camera zoomed in and focused on Suk-Jun's handsome face. Suk-Jun's deeply rouged eyes swelled with horror.

"What's going on here?" Kyung-A seemed thoroughly confused. "He's the hero! That's not supposed to happen!" She had her sudden doubt. "Is it?"

She looked to Kwang-Chul for an explanation. He simply shrugged his shoulders. Kyung-A turned and looked around Glade for someone to say something, but no one was paying any attention.

The scene froze and the end credits rolled while a merry little tune, the show's theme music, loudly played.

On the opposite side of the bar, Chan-Woo reached for the universal remote and shut off the television. Punching another button, he turned on the stereo sound system. A lively beat immediately reverberated throughout Glade.

Deep in thought, Kwang-Chul hung his head down. He felt a stab out of the past. The whole scene had seemed familiar to him, as if he should know it. He tried to hold onto the thought to see where it would lead him, but it was gone in an instant. He swiveled in his seat and looked inquiringly around, as if he could locate its source. Glade's warm lights and convivial atmosphere wrapped his senses in comforting familiarity.

Shrugging off the feeling of déjà vu, he set his misgivings aside and unthinkingly tapped his shoe to the funky music permeating the establishment.

Doubt tore at Yoo-Min's heart. She clawed at her thighs, forlorn with the thought that Suk-Jun didn't love her after all.

Grabbing some clothes, she dressed hurriedly for work and caught the train for It'aewon-dong. The green and white train left the station and rocketed through the subway tube, exploding into the summer night. A light drizzle was falling upon Seoul. The streets scintillated with an opalescent sheen.

Gazing out the window, Yoo-Min mindlessly watched the passing scenery whiz by in a watery blur – streets crowded with automobiles spewing their invisible toxic fumes; pedestrians of all shapes and ages milling on the sidewalks, sweltering in the humidity; gargantuan television screens advertising the latest fashions and cosmetic products and the newest soft drinks peddled by image-conscious pop divas from the gleaming façades of huge glass and steel edifices; a panoply of neon signs and bright posters and washed-out billboards; restaurants, multi-storied department stores, stone-faced government buildings; light poles, telephone poles, electrical poles with thick black wires stretching in all directions into infinity.

Arriving in It'aewon-dong, she made her way through the rows of eateries and drinking houses until she came to Glade. The dingy entrance with its pink neon light and windows with thick, purple velvet curtains to shut out the view gave her pause. She had no idea how she had come to work at Glade. Something had pulled her there, some mysterious force she could not fathom. She wondered:

Did fate bring me here just so I could meet Suk-Jun?

Inside, the atmosphere reeked of cigarette smoke and cheap booze. Sexy girls in black, tight-fitting dresses slinked about like wild cats on the prowl. Groups of white-shirted men with their sleeves rolled up and ties unknotted sat drinking at contemporary aluminum bar tables in the center of the room below a multifaceted disco ball that cast a tessellated pattern over the dark interior. A few of the hostesses perched with the customers, smiling at them with their painted lips and black pearl eyes while they poured soju and whiskey and feigned attentiveness.

Spotting an empty table, Yoo-Min flopped onto a chair, making sure that a clear view was afforded of her legs. Carefully scanning the room, she saw that there was no one of any consequence in the place, no one capable of evoking the slightest interest in her. An amethyst-eyed hostess with blood-red fingernails and vampire black hair slithered up and brought her a glass of soju. She sipped it leisurely. A group of drunken businessmen and several of the hostesses were horse dancing to *Gangnam Style*. Her thoughts meandered and she slipped effortlessly into a fugue.

After awhile she made up her mind to leave early. She had already consumed three glasses of soju; she was immensely bored and feeling drunk. The room closed in on her; she longed to be home.

Suddenly she caught sight of Kwang-Chul, the owner's son, gaping at her from across the room. She felt uncomfortable when he did not take his eyes off her. Startled by the boldness of his gaze, she thought:

Why, that little creep is looking right at me.

As far as she was concerned, someone as unremarkable looking as Kwang-Chul had no right staring at her in such a manner – or in any manner, for that matter. Under any other circumstances, she would have glared at him angrily.

113

But she was unable to do so. As she turned to face him, he stared unblinkingly into her eyes. His eyes were fixed, motionless, almost rapturous with a religious fervor, as if they had spotted their heaven. For one prolonged moment, the unspoken contact between them was unyielding.

Suddenly his eyes seemed to look right through her, and not just at her, as if they had fixed in their sight some distant, buried, innermost part of her. The awareness that he had penetrated almost to the core of her being was unsettling. No one had ever looked at her in that way before. The look in those eyes was almost vulgar in its uncanny ability to pierce right through her and chart her deepest waters. The thought crossed her mind:

The way you look at me, I feel like we've known each other for centuries. But that's impossible.

The corners of his mouth showed the vaguest hint of a smile, while his eyes, holding hers, seemed to dreamily intone: *I want you more than anything else in the world.*

She leapt from her seat and indignantly marched across the room to confront him.

"Don't look at me like that!" she demanded angrily.

"How do I look at you?" he asked, his face blanched with embarrassment.

"With such a look," she said fiercely.

"I don't know what you mean," he said, backpedaling away from her.

She aggressively pursued him into a corner. She observed that his mouth was nervously twitching – a sure sign that he was lying – and this only angered her more.

"You know exactly what I mean! The way a man looks at the woman he loves, as if she's the only woman in the world for him, as if he's found his heaven. You have no right to look at me in that way!"

"I didn't look at you like that!"

"You did! You do so even now!" she accused him flatly. "I can see it in your eyes! You want me! Every man wants me!" Her almond eyes narrowed to fierce slits. "Don't you ever look at me in that way! You're too ugly to look at me like that!" she cried, throwing up her arms in disgust and watching pleased as the life went out in his eyes.

And then *he* appeared. Suk-Jun. He caught her eye the moment he strolled through the door. He was wearing a black silk shirt and double pleated linen pants. His thick black hair was slicked back with a greaseless gel. His eyes were like opulent jade green beads. Suk-Jun was so stunningly gorgeous, his looks were almost mythic. Dressed to kill, he was every bit the kind of man she had long dreamed of.

Several hostesses rushed up to greet him with admiring eyes and porcelain smiles. Yoo-Min fumed as they fawned over him like obsequious maidservants. She became even more vexed when he didn't seem to mind.

A few minutes later he strolled jauntily up, reeking of self-assurance. He said hello but she pretended not to notice him. Through lowered lashes she watched him reach into his pocket and withdraw a pack of cigarettes.

"Smoke?" he asked, offering her the pack.

"Sure," she said in a hollow voice after a moment's hesitation, just long enough to allow recognition to flicker in her eyes. She didn't smoke, but she didn't want to refuse his offer. She took the pack of cigarettes from his hand and lightly tapped one out, wryly noting that they were

Pyongyang cigarettes. Slipping it between her lips, she mumbled, "Light?"

Suk-Jun pulled a satin silver finish torch flame lighter from his jacket pocket and flicked its lever to ignite the torch flame. She leaned forward and let the tip of the cigarette touch the bluish flame. She sucked briefly on the other end without inhaling, just enough for the tip to glow bright red. Satisfied, she took the cigarette from her lips with two slender fingers and leaned back and let her almond eyes linger on his.

She could feel Suk-Jun's animal magnetism exerting its pull. Keeping her cool, she exhaled and watched through slit eyes as the smoke lazily curled upwards.

"Thanks."

She handed the pack of Pyongyang cigarettes back to him. The touch of his satin fingertips sent hot flashes down her spine and she accidentally dropped the pack. Before she could make a move to retrieve it, Kwang-Chul suddenly appeared out of nowhere.

"I'll find it!" she heard him call as he dove beneath the table and scrambled about on his hands and knees.

She took another puff from her cigarette and inhaled the smoke deeply into her lungs. At once she began to choke and cough – the room briefly spun around and finally settled on Suk-Jun's bemused face.

"You look green," he said, reaching over to lightly pat her back. "Better take it easy."

Furious with herself, she exerted supreme self-control and willed herself to stop coughing. She saw Kwang-Chul on all fours with his head almost between her legs. An ugly black mole on the top of his balding head caught her eye. She touched it with the tip of her cigarette.

"Ouch! Hey, watch it!"

She laughed as the table shook when he banged his head on its underside. Her eyes danced in the scintillating light as he angrily flipped the pack of cigarettes on the table and then mercifully banished himself from her sight.

"You haven't called me," she said sulkily to Suk-Jun, thrusting her lower lip out into a pout.

Suk-Jun turned a chair around and straddled it, folding his arms across the back of the chair. "I'm sorry," he said. The features of his face drooped in a display of contriteness.

She couldn't decide whether he was being sincere. His eyes shone brightly, hardly a sign of feeling sorry for one's actions. But when he flashed a disarming smile, she decided at once that all was forgiven. She gazed upon him with a look meant to convey absolution.

Flagging a hostess, Suk-Jun ordered a bottle of Jinro Gold. It came in a stainless steel diamond cut ice bucket with two old fashioned glasses and slices of lemon. Yoo-Min meticulously prepared two lemon sojus on the rocks. She handed one to Suk-Jun and watched as he swirled the soju and ice around in his glass before drinking it half down. She followed suit, sipping her drink leisurely.

"A lot of women don't like the taste of soju," he remarked, nodding with appreciation. "They say it's like drinking ethanol."

"I love it," she said. She was pleased by his approval. Her chest heaved as the soju warmed her, and she stroked her thighs provocatively.

They chatted amicably for awhile. Suk-Jun ordered octopus heads and they gorged themselves. When the soju had sufficiently dulled her inhibitions, Yoo-Min looked around and seeing that all the booths were occupied, said, "Follow me."

Grabbing Suk-Jun by the hand, she led him into one of the two bathrooms in the back of Glade. The stench of urine and cigarette smoke was strong. Kicking the door shut with her heel, she waited for him to make his move.

She expected him to do something. In fact, she expected him to rape her – wasn't that the natural thing to do? What recourse would she have but to prove to him that there was no sweeter pleasure in the world than the pleasure she could give him, no greater sacrifice she could make than to give herself to him completely and wholeheartedly?

Groping frantically for his jaji, she pleaded hotly in his ear: "Give it to me, Suk-Jun. Give it to me now. I'll do whatever you want."

She fell to her knees and grabbed his jaji and held it reverently between her hands. It squirmed like an immense writhing serpent in the muted light; it took both her hands just to hold onto it. It was a magnificent specimen of manhood, one no doubt capable of plumbing her depths and pleasuring her into a state of unspeakable madness. She had never seen anything like it. Her eyes lit upon its umbrella-shaped tip in utter fascination. Her pupils widened as the pieces of the puzzle began abruptly falling into place. Her thoughts raced back to So-Yun's cryptic remark earlier in the day: *You will know him by his mark.* There it was, on the tip of his jaji, plain as day, a perse birthmark in the amorphous shape of a Rorschach inkblot. She ecstatically thought: *He's the one!*

Suddenly it was as if the floodgates of her emotions had opened. Furiously stroking his jaji, she burst into a recital of her apprehensions. She told Suk-Jun about her memories of having lived another life a long time ago and how she had been loved by a boy named Han-Yong. She told him how she had spurned Han-Yong because of her vanity and pride,

118

and how he had taken on the vows of a monk to forget about his love for her. Then she told him that she loved Han-Yong and would always love Han-Yong, and she knew that Han-Yong would always love her, that they were destined to be together because they were soul mates, two souls fashioned out of one. Finally, she cried:

"Suk-Jun, don't you understand? You and Han-Yong are one and the same!"

"That's ridiculous, Yoo-Min! It's just your imagination! It's not real!"

"It's not my imagination! I know it's not!" she cried fiercely. Her heart was aching with the fury of a love that had gone unfulfilled for centuries. "You must believe me! I'm the only one for you and you're the only one for me!"

Was there a spark of recognition in Suk-Jun's eyes? Surely Suk-Jun knew, surely he could see beyond the pale of the present and divine the truth of their eternal love! Yes, she could see it in his eyes. *He knows*, she thought wildly. She fairly swooned with joy. Suk-Jun was speaking to her. She couldn't hear his words. It was as if the sound of his voice had traveled a great distance, a distance measured not by space but by time, not by years but by centuries. The words themselves were lost in time. His voice emanated not from the odorous confines of the urine-soaked bathroom in Glade where in her besotted frenzy she clung to his jaji for dear life, but from somewhere mysterious and unfathomable, from the vast depths of her soul perhaps.

"You're crazy!"

"What are you saying?"

"Leave me alone! Take your hands off me!"

"Don't say that!"

"Get away from me!" Suk-Jun shouted, tearing her hands from his jaji and tucking it in his pants.

"What do you mean, you won't have me? My boji isn't good enough for you?" She lashed out at him with her fists. Tears of rage streamed down her face.

And then she saw Kwang-Chul framed in the doorway of the bathroom. His ochreous face floated like a jaundiced moon in a miasma of smoke and gloom. He had witnessed the whole scene.

"Get out of here! Mind your own business!"

She waved him off but it was too late. Suk-Jun stormed out of the bathroom without so much as a look at her.

When Suk-Jun either would not fulfill his manly duty, the rejection she had felt hurt her more than any pain he could give her. When she finally emerged from the bathroom looking like a wounded bird, she felt completely defeated.

Later that night after she had returned home, she frenetically paced her room. She didn't know what to do with herself. Thinking of the way that creep Kwang-Chul had looked at her earlier that evening, she felt icicles pricking her veins. No one had ever looked at her in that way, not even Suk-Jun.

She clenched her fists in silent fury. She wanted a real man, a man who would make fierce love to her every night. She needed to feel his manhood penetrating to the core of her being, to know with her flesh that he really did love her, for only through the intimate discourse of their bodies would the truth be revealed.

She walked over to the window and drew back the curtains. The tepid night lay opaque outside her window. Drops of rain splattered against the glass; a storm was brewing. She slowly undressed and stood naked in the center of the room. She pressed the palms of her hands to her breasts and cupped them. Her hands were cold and their coldness against her nipples sent shivers through her flesh.

She closed her eyes as her lingering fingers inflamed her lurid thoughts. But the uncertainty she felt about Suk-Jun was greater than her fleeting desire, and she savagely whipped her head back in pain.

Then she cast herself onto her yo and stared emptily into space, feeling her essence melt into the shadows.

Yoo-Min lay on her yo listening to the blustery din outside her window. An unnatural wind was sweeping through Seoul. Clutching her pillow, her eyes widened as a sudden gust slammed against the panes. Picturing all sorts of evil outside her window, she snapped her eyes tight, hoping to shut them out.

As if some benevolent god of nature had heard and obeyed her will, there was an abrupt lull in the commotion outdoors. In the ensuing peace, the world outside her window seemed especially desolate and sorrowful, as if her own sad barrenness had somehow managed to foist itself upon nature. But then, as she mulled over this thought, its ridiculousness struck her. How could the empty silence outside possibly compare with the devastating bleakness of her own existence?

Yoo-Min longed for upheaval in her world. She longed for the day when someone would enter her life and sweep her off her feet, just like in one of those pulp magazines she read by the stack. But the storm she longed for never came. Instead her days and nights were filled with mind-numbing regularity.

Most nights she undressed and lay naked on her yo and imagined herself in the arms of the man she loved. The man she envisioned was always a dazzling heroic figure imbued with glory and virtue and, of course, irrepressible good looks. On nights like these she felt herself whole. Delighting in the sensations of her heightened senses, and surrendering herself completely, she loathed the moment when she would have to snap out of her reverie.

But these glossy compositions of unreality invariably left her feeling unsatisfied and wanting. Dreams alone could not fulfill her. Nature had given her a woman's body and with it came the awareness that her happiness was ultimately rooted in her flesh, and this because a woman's body was ineluctably linked to a man's. She needed to feel the continuity of flesh between herself and a man, to sense the unity between the disparate parts, thigh and hip, breast and hand, to be conscious of her body as a piece of fabric interwoven with another piece of fabric – only then could the emptiness which plagued her be driven away, or at least mitigated. Her heart burst into spasms of yearning for the warm happiness she instinctively knew would flow through every cell in her body when a man proved himself between the soft, yielding flesh of her thighs. After all, she asked herself, wasn't this the secret yearning of women everywhere?

There were darker fantasies, too. Secretly she believed that she didn't deserve to know this kind of happiness. Sometimes when her spirits were especially low, she imagined herself forced to watch the man of her dreams make love to another woman. But was it pangs of pleasure or pain she felt whenever she dwelt upon such images? Certainly she derived some twisted satisfaction from the torment she gave herself.

Yoo-Min had long surmised that she had masochistic tendencies. How else could she explain her willingness to be mistreated by the men in her life, like Suk-Jun for instance? Before meeting Suk-Jun, she had been afraid of her own sexuality and had to test it out on other women. But these had been harmless flirtations and nothing more.

Was there ever a darker time in her life? Her heart surged with the uncertain memories of her past. An unclear recollection, long dormant, struggled to make itself known. In a haze, she dimly saw her father standing naked over her mother, his jaji proud and erect, his hand clenched white with rage. The powerful sunlight pouring in through the window set him aglow with a golden hue. The whole time Sook-Sun sobbed in her pillow, her nude body flushed with distress and humiliation and marred with evidence of Ki-Yul's brutality. Through her long eyelashes, Yoo-Min contemplated her father's hardy features and decided that he was quite handsome. His distant forebears were from beyond the northern slope of the Taebaek mountains. There were traces of war-like ancestry in his face. Eyes gorged with satisfaction, she encouraged him:

"Beat her, Daddy! Beat her good!"

Though streaked with crimson, her mother's breasts were shockingly beautiful; she hated them and longed to see them disfigured.

"If you won't do it, I will!" she cried, lunging for a thick leather belt on the dresser.

"Get out of here!" Ki-Yul bellowed, kicking her in the ass and sending her scurrying from the room. "Mind your own business!"

Reflecting upon the distant past, Yoo-Min stirred restlessly upon her yo. Many years before, on a bright, beautiful, sunny spring day, as she was slipping into her school uniform, her mother appeared at the door of her room with a tall, sallow-faced stranger. Blushing the color of cherry blossoms, she hurriedly pulled up her skirt and fastened her belt.

"The doctor's here to give you an examination," said her mother in a voice ringing with false sincerity. "Take off your clothes."

But there was more of the criminal than the clinical about the sinister looking man who entered the room and set a black leather bag on the ondol floor. Protesting that she wasn't in the least bit sick, she made for the door. Her mother quickly blocked her exit. Just then the stranger must have come up behind her and administered some sort of anesthetic, for suddenly she was overcome with grogginess.

Struggling futilely, she was unable to resist as they lay her down on her yo. Through a haze, she watched horrified as the unsavory doctor unpacked an array of shiny instruments from the black leather bag and arranged them in a neat little row on a white cotton cloth he had fastidiously spread on the floor. When he finished, he turned to her with an unmistakable leer and lifted up her pleated skirt, slithering his rough hands up her lily thighs and stripping off her white cotton panties. She wanted to die from humiliation when he began examining the hollow of her groin, probing it with his thick, calloused forefinger. She felt the throbbing, pulsing rhythm of her blood as the pressure increased, and saw her mother turn her head so as not to witness the assault. Her head began to swim; she felt a cold numbness between her legs. Finally she watched in soundless fascination as he held a platinum silver ring up to the light and with a callous grin placed it against her boji. It was then that the true horror of her situation struck her.

"It's for your own good. You'll understand when you get older," her mother sought to reassure her as she fiercely struggled to escape. But the effects of the numbing agent she had been administered rendered her powerless to do so.

She decided to murder her mother. Her plan was simple and therefore elegant. Each night before bed Sook-Sun enjoyed a cup of hot tea spiced with ginseng root and other healing herbs; Yoo-Min decided to administer a lethal dose of sleeping medication to her mother's herbal brew. Everyone knew that Sook-Sun was prone to bouts of depression. They would reasonably conclude that her death was a suicide.

On the night she chose to carry out her plan, her mother intended to soak in a hot bath, as Sook-Sun always did when the weather turned cold. Yoo-Min offered to make her mother a cup of tea with the usual medicinal ingredients. Sook-Sun didn't suspect a thing. She pleasantly agreed and sauntered off to bathe.

"Can you do my back first?" Sook-Sun called over her shoulder in a voice as soft as morning virga. "And then you can make the tea."

"Sure," Yoo-Min said, following her mother into the bathroom. She watched enviously as her mother slipped off her pink silk robe and stood naked in front of the tub like a graceful crane. Her mother's slender figure was pale and delicate and almost too ethereal to be real.

Sook-Sun showered before stepping into the tub to soak. She plunged her face into the spraying water and wet her long black hair. Drawing the strands of hair back from her face, she reached for a bar of perfumed soap and handed it to Yoo-Min.

"Here."

Yoo-Min took the soap and vigorously scrubbed her mother's back. The skin turned crimson from the rubbing.

Sook-Sun lowered her eyelashes and contentedly purred, "Ah, that feels wonderful!"

Yoo-Min wiped the sweat from her brow with the back of her hand. Completing the task, she gave the soap back to her mother. Sook-Sun took the occasion to look her full in the face. No words were exchanged, but an understanding of some nature passed between them. The sadness in Sook-Sun's eyes was unmistakable. Had she some prescience of her fate? Yoo-Min turned away uncomfortably.

"I'll go make the tea," she said almost fiercely.

Undaunted, she dashed to the kitchen. Her feet were wet and she nearly slipped and fell. She put a kettle of water on the stove to heat. The ethereal sound of a ch'ojok filled the air. Her mother must have turned on a radio. She spilled the contents of a bottle of her mother's sleeping pills onto a sheet of white paper on the kitchen table. A dozen yellow pills, each the size of a sunflower seed, fanned across the paper. Adrenaline surged through her body as she sensed the latent potency of each pill. *Seeds of death*, she thought ecstatically. With a pestle used for crushing walnuts, she pulverized the pills into a fine powder . . .

The clamoring wind startled Yoo-Min; she drew in her breath sharply. She realized that her chest was laboring; her breasts heaved and shook like young jellyfish. But the roar in her ears was really the garrulity of her own thoughts. She was still at a complete loss as to what really happened that night . . .

She had been on the verge of dumping the powder into her mother's tea cup and mixing it up with a teaspoon when she had a sudden change of heart. *How can I kill my own mother?* What happened after that was a mystery. She vaguely remembered trudging back to her room and collapsing on her yo in a fit of despondency. She must have fallen asleep after that, for sometime later her father came bursting into her room with the terrible news.

"Wake up, Yoo-Min!"

A hand was shaking her roughly by the shoulder.

"Huh? What?"

"Something tragic has happened."

"What?" Instantly her mind was alert. Even before her father spoke, she had an inkling as to what he was going to say.

"Your mother's dead," he told her coldly.

"What did you say?" The pronouncement shrieked in her brain like the pitiful cry of a mortally wounded creature. "*No-ooo!*"

He drew her head against her shoulder and held it there with his hand to comfort her.

"She fell asleep in the bath and drowned."

Upon hearing this, Yoo-Min had plunged into a sea of numbness, as if every nerve in her body had been pierced with acupuncture needles. Her whole body threatened to collapse and extinguish itself in darkness. But the consoling presence of her father who curled up beside her gave her the strength to live. Later, in the solitude of her room, she undid the terrible thing that had been done to her.

She was vindicated on that altogether uncommon night. Or, in the throes of despair, had she imagined everything? The mystery of that night deepened when, the following morning, she could not find the sleeping powder she had made. She was certain that she had dumped it into the trash, but it was no longer there. Had she given it to her mother after all? Years later, she never really knew whether she had dreamt the whole thing or not.

She was fifteen years old when her mother died. Without warning, the bright happiness she had known as a child quickly dimmed and transformed into an inner darkness. Then, too, the world seemed a perilous place for a young girl poised on the brink of becoming a woman. The grasping, manipulating ways of her girlfriends, the easy alliances between boys and girls, the numerous deceits and treacheries – all of these augured the approaching storms of adulthood.

With her forefinger, Yoo-Min wiped a corner of her eye. Throughout the years there was one hope she clung to, one luminous ray capable of dispelling the murkiness which engulfed her. This was the hope of a love so strong and consuming that it would transfuse the darkness of her world with radiance. Without love, there was no life. Without love, there was only interminable emptiness.

She lay quietly listening to the pounding rains pummeling Seoul. Now that the storm had arrived, her fears were somewhat allayed. The storm's tangibleness was a known and comprehensible factor compared to the frightening abstractions of her imagination.

Clenching her ibul, she wondered if Suk-Jun felt a storm in his heart at that very moment. Was it as powerful as the tempest outside her window? Her hand restlessly glided up the smooth skin of her belly and gently cupped her breast. Under her ibul, she dug her fingers into her thighs, knotting them tremulously and burying them deep in her flesh. In the unmoving darkness, the whites of her eyes flashed. She whimpered just a little at the intimacy of her feverish thoughts.

As she drifted towards sleep, she discerned an indistinct figure moving towards her in a shadowy world of unreality, a dark, nebulous figure she had glimpsed several times before in the turbid night, always as she was on the verge of some marvelous, shimmering dream unlike any other.

That night Kwang-Chul lay desiring to sleep but he was unable to do so. The little yellow capsules he had taken, guaranteed to lull the dragons of the mind, had not worked. He read the tale of King Mu and Pangjang; it evoked longings in him. Then he sat facing a wall for almost an hour. He was completely fatigued, but still he could not sleep.

It was almost four o'clock in the morning. He heard the shuffle of his mother's padded slippers on the ondol floor as she went to her room and prepared for bed. The walls were not thick and the ensuing silence ensured him that she was asleep.

He kept thinking about Yoo-Min. She had shown up at Glade that evening and immediately made a wanton display of herself in a provocatively short tiffany blue dress, exhibiting her long wispy legs for everyone to see. The sight of her making a spectacle of herself was more than he could bear.

Not only that, but she had caught him ogling her and proceeded to berate him in front of everyone. He had felt thoroughly humiliated. Even his mother had heaped scorn upon him. She had witnessed the whole scene and had stormed up to him afterwards, throwing these very words in his face: "Have you lost your dignity as a man?"

To make matters worse, who else should suddenly show up at Glade that evening but that rascal Suk-Jun! It didn't take Suk-Jun long at all to home in on Yoo-Min. He had just about died when he saw her escort Suk-Jun into the bathroom. Jumping to his feet, he had intended to check out the situation but his mother blocked his way. "Leave them alone," she ordered him. "He'll pay extra for this!"

As if that wasn't enough, later in the evening Suk-Jun commenced to charm his mother with his suave manners and glib talk. Kwang-Chul nearly puked with disgust. But that wasn't all. Oh no, not by a long shot! To add insult to injury, Suk-Jun had pointed to his mid-thigh and laughingly proclaimed, "It's *this* big!" Kyung-A, smashed on six glasses of soju, *oohed* and *aahed* like a doting schoolgirl. All the while Kwang-Chul had stood by and watched in silent rage – a pathetic, impotent puppy.

Drawing back the curtains of his window, Kwang-Chul peered through the glass. He wondered, as he pressed his face against the windowpane and watched as his breath fogged the glass, "Is she asleep now?"

With his forefinger, he traced a line on the misted-over windowpane and stared through it into the night without really seeing anything. He wanted her safe at home and most definitely alone. But what if she were not alone? What if she were with *him?* As visions of Yoo-Min naked in the arms of Suk-Jun hammered in his brain, he bitterly thought: *Then she should die.*

Kwang-Chul felt his conscience stabbing at him like acupuncture needles. The purity he longed for in his heart seemed small and insignificant compared with the immensity of his desire for Yoo-Min. Yet his desire for her stood in complete contraposition to his deepest aspirations. He wished he could yank out his desire by the root, pluck it from his body and cast it away as in the biblical admonition, rather than have his vision obscured. He shut the lids of his eyes tight. Meditate! He must meditate more! Was it not said that meditation was the only path to enlightenment? Did not Hyujŏng state that the clean purity of the mind is Buddha? And did not Pou in his *Il Chŏng* say that when the mind of man is pure, the mind of the universe is also pure,

131

and if the ki within man is consonant with the one true reality, likewise the ki of the universe is consonant with the one true reality? And was it not said that he who seeks perfection must constantly struggle against his emotions? And was it not also said that perfection may be likened to a parting of the clouds of the mind so that the flawless blue sky of one's true nature is revealed?

The clouds of Kwang-Chul's mind were dark, troublesome, and unyielding.

Oh, but Yoo-Min bedeviled him so! His spirit yearned for her in the way a man yearns for his god; his flesh longed for her in the way a man longs for an ordinary whore. There could be no peace in his heart so long as she would not love him. And if she would not love him, then, by the breath of Buddha, he must take his pleasure from her as a man would take his pleasure from any woman, for what was the difference between the agonizing joy he would feel upon ravishing her body to his heart's content and the blissful torment he would endure in loving her without the slightest hope of ever being loved in return? They were one and the same.

He lay in the darkness absorbing the sounds and sensations of the night. The silence was portentous. He could almost hear the perturbations of his karma expanding outward and exponentially amplifying, reaching into the past, present, and future, and interacting with the karma of others.

Struggling to make sense out of the tangled web of thoughts that teased his brain, he inexorably drifted into sleep.

Something woke him.

Propping himself on an elbow, Kwang-Chul looked outside and saw that the rain showers that had soaked Seoul all evening had dissipated.

Pressing his nose against the window, he felt troubled by a vague apprehension. What had disturbed the calm of the night? Was it merely the wind whipping against his windowpane? Slipping out of bed, he tiptoed in his bare feet across the ondol floor and cautiously opened his bedroom door. He peered into the stultifying blackness. No one was there.

His ears pricked up at the sound of a muted cry.

Suspicion stabbed at his heart. Hushed voices came from his mother's room. His mother was not alone.

Fear and loathing raged inside his heart like twin typhoons. Creeping up to her room, he saw that the door was open just a crack. A thin sliver of light streaming from the room streaked the ondol floor outside the door. He put his eye up to the crack.

On the edge of the bed, illuminated by pearly moonlight pouring through the window, was a young man of immense muscularity. Kwang-Chul knew who it was immediately: Suk-Jun. Suk-Jun was sitting with his naked back to the door, a back as broad and rippling as a large barrel. Massive, square shoulders supported an enormous head, and a thick tangle of hair like jungle vines covered the nape. His mother was sitting upright on the bed, leaning back on her arms. To his dismay, she didn't have a stitch of clothing on. Legs crossed, she seemed relaxed, as if she were having tea with an old friend.

"Ah!" Kyung-A cried suddenly, throwing up her delicate hands. Horrified, Kwang-Chul's first thought was that she had seen him. But he was mistaken: her cry was one of delight. He watched stupefied as Suk-Jun's huge jaji reared its swollen head above a tangled sea of black hair, like a magnificent creature rising out of a dark sea, while his mother, the playful nymph, worshipped it like a god.

Suddenly Suk-Jun seized her like a doll and laid her on her back and moved silently atop her. From the twisted, knotted hair between his legs, his glorious jaji, capable of ripping the seams of reality wide open, brandished itself above the soft, rippling fields of her flesh. Kyung-A's swelling breasts caught the moonlight. Her pale skin shimmered with sweat.

Mesmerized, Kwang-Chul was thrilled just to watch. Suk-Jun had muscles that were hard and thick, bulging veins that were taut like steel cable. Kwang-Chul was awed by Suk-Jun's manly performance and thought that his mother was equally splendid. Transformed by passion, she was scarcely recognizable to him.

Abruptly Suk-Jun turned his head and stared directly at the door, riveting his gaze on the crack where Kwang-Chul's eye was glued. Kwang-Chul froze stiff with terror. Surely Suk-Jun's eyes were on him now, surely they had seen him peering through the crack! Those powerful eyes held him with their dark, riveting stare. Kwang-Chul felt his will dissolve into nothingness. Suk-Jun's eyes would not let him go.

"It hurts!" Kyung-A cried suddenly. "You're hurting me!"

Suk-Jun turned his immense head and gazed at the doll-like figure writhing beneath him. The spell was instantly broken.

Tearing himself away from the door, Kwang-Chul stumbled and fell to the ondol floor. He scrambled to his room on all fours and collapsed on his bed. His emotions raged like a buk sori. How dare his mother let Suk-Jun occupy her bed and defile her sheets! In his anguish and confusion he toppled out of bed.

"What's going on in there?"

His mother's knock on the door brought him to his senses. He cursed himself under his breath and smacked himself soundly on the side of his head for good measure. Scrambling back into bed, he called out in a casual voice:

"Nothing! Everything's fine!"

"It sounded like a fight in there!"

"I was having a nightmare! I fell out of bed!"

"Well, you'd better be careful!" his mother admonished him from outside the door. "Now go back to sleep!"

Smothering his head in his pillow, Kwang-Chul closed his eyes and struggled to contain his thoughts. His thoughts whipped and hurled and beat upon the walls of his head like a furious tempest. They roared. They descended upon him with unrelenting fury. They would not cease. They nearly drove him mad.

Gripping his pillow, he hung on for dear life. At last the storm in his head subsided. Soaked with sweat and feeling utterly exhausted, and with his face buried in his pillow, he conjured up Yoo-Min's image in his thoughts and fixed it there, and then plunged headlong into sleep.

Yoo-Min woke up with a start and felt her entire body blanch with fear. Her heart was pounding frantically, as it sometimes did when she woke up from a disturbing dream. She caught her breath as her heart missed a beat or two. She had a momentary sinking feeling, as if she were on a plummeting elevator. She realized that she was sweating profusely. Her breasts gleamed with perspiration.

No one was there. But something was wrong. She felt a persistent cramp in her abdomen and wondered if her overdue period was finally coming. She lay on her back waiting for the cramps to subside, but they didn't. They increased in intensity until she couldn't stand the discomfort any longer. She felt the pressure in her abdomen encircling her and tightening like a steel band, followed by a sharp pain and then, without warning, a gush of blood from between her legs.

She turned on a light and examined her sheet. It was stained with blood. She felt faint, suspecting at once what it might be. The realization that the life within her was gone was more than she could endure. She threw herself on her yo and buried her head in her pillow and sobbed uncontrollably, while between sobs the questions screamed from her lips:

"Why? Why me? What have I done? My baby, oh, my baby!"

Blurry-eyed with tears, she tore the sheet from her yo and left it crumpled on the floor. She lay back on her yo and closed her eyes in unremitting pain. The pain was greater than she could bear; it had never been this bad before. There was no way to stop it, no way to put an end to the

136

onslaught of despair. Her loneliness was overwhelming. She felt that she was going insane.

Was it all her imagination as Suk-Jun had said? Was there never a time when she had lived beneath the slope of a large mountain, never a time when she had been loved by a boy named Han-Yong, never a night long ago, a night forever lost in time, when she had encountered Han-Yong on a path in the forest under a star-encrusted sky? Why hadn't Han-Yong saved her? Had there never been a Jung-Sin to save?

"I'm not imagining things," she cried, tightly holding onto her pillow as if to confirm its existence. "It's all real, it must be real."

There was only one thing to do. Frantically tearing her hair, she ran into the bathroom and emerged moments later clutching a bottle of pills in one hand and a glass of water in the other. Ripping off the cap, she poured out a number of pills and popped them into her mouth. She took several gulps of water and swallowed more than once and felt the pills go down one by one.

Just like my mother, she thought with a sadness that was unbearable.

"More," she mumbled, filling her mouth with another handful of pills and swallowing them all.

She lay on her yo and shut her eyes. As the pills worked their way through her system, her limbs felt shod with lead.

She suddenly opened her eyes.

"I know you are here," she said. "I can feel you."

The emptiness of the room smothered her. Silence roared in her ears like the thunderous waters of Cheonjiyeon.

"Do you – want me?"

She could feel her heart pound like the fervent beat of a changgo drum.

"Do you — love me?"

Quick as thought, he was there. She felt him press his face against her cheek. His lips sucked tenderly at her eyelids. His unseen hands sought her breasts. Her breasts rose up to meet them and submit themselves to his touch. Every nerve in her body shrieked with ineffable desire, every cell screamed for death to release it from its impossible torment.

His lips pressed fiercely down on hers. She instantly plunged into a fathomless sea of pleasure. The softness of his lips, their delicious moistness, his tongue quivering like seaweed in her mouth — sensations too indefinable, too exquisite to be real. She was convinced that she was dreaming.

As he glided effortlessly between her legs, she knew that no dream was ever this real.

"Oh my God," she moaned. "What are you doing to me?"

He did not answer her.

"Love me," she seethed, fiercely digging her nails into his shoulders. "Love me."

He did. He made love to her as she had longed to be made love to for so many nights. Her body moved in cadence with his own, absorbing him inexorably and utterly; she was one with him.

"Don't stop," she implored. "Please don't stop."

The whites of her eyes shone with unabated pleasure. "So good," she breathed, and her body drew him closer still, pulled him even deeper into her own. "Feels so good."

She shuddered with rapture as the seething sensations of his jaji unfurled across her mind. She submitted herself completely as he filled the emptiness of her being with his own essence. The commingling of her nature and his gave rise in her a sense of wholeness she had never experienced until that moment.

"Who are you?" she murmured softly. "Show yourself to me."

As the morning's first light filtered through the window, she discerned through half-closed eyes an indefinite figure, a faintly perceptible form scarcely distinguishable from the hazy shadows of the room, and she dimly thought:

And then like a Hanwha skyrocket bursting across the night sky over Hangang Park, the realization exploded across her mind:

Kwallŭk!

Kwang-Chul was awakened by the rays of the early morning sun stabbing at his eyes. His sheet was drenched with sweat and clung to his skin, producing a dappled pattern against his chest. He felt immensely drained. With his eyes half-closed, he vaguely wondered: *Am I awake or am I dreaming?*

The reality of his room seemed pale and vitiated – a mere abstraction when compared to the lustrous reality of his dream. Usually drab and colorless, his room appeared even more so. And the early morning sunshine bursting through his window seemed especially lackluster.

Tugging at his sheet, he drew it up to his neck. His thoughts materialized out of a dense fog like ships upon a misty sea, only to disappear once again into the nebulous haze. He felt as if he were under the influence of some kind of drug. The superb clarity of consciousness he had experienced during the night was gone. He told himself: *I must be dreaming. I'll probably wake up any moment now.*

Shutting his eyes, Kwang-Chul lay listening to the gentle, reassuring sound of his own breathing. His eyelids fluttered, opened a hair's breadth, closed again. As he settled into that twilight state between wakefulness and sleep, everything seemed peaceful and calm. It was not. Wavering between realms of shadow and light, Kwang-Chul became sluggishly aware of an opaqueness at the foot of his bed – a depth of blackness in the uncertain shape of a man. The thought flashed across his mind:

Suk-Jun.

The blackness drifted over him like a summer squall and hovered above his chest, threatening to demolish his precarious existence. He had the vague notion that the

140

world ceased to exist within this tenebrous depth. Its impenetrable darkness signaled danger, even death. Chaos never loomed so large. Horrified, he thought: *Is this the emptiness of my own soul?*

Shaking off the vestiges of sleep, Kwang-Chul bolted upright in bed. Nothing was there. It had been his imagination, pure and simple. He told himself:

It was only a dream.

He lay down again and closed his eyes and listened to the vigorous pounding of his heart. After awhile his heartbeat became subdued and his breath grew shallow, while the familiar matutinal sounds outside his window lulled his senses into a wonderful quiescence. The rhythms of life oscillated with an ineffable beauty that only his inner senses could discern.

His mother's voice chimed outside his bedroom door. "Kwang-Chul! Breakfast!"

"Be right there!"

Slipping into a pair of jeans and buckling his belt, he strolled into the kitchen and sniffed the savory aromas there.

"Have a seat," his mother said affectionately, tousling his hair.

He flopped onto a pillow in front of the low dining table. Bowls of rice and egg, kimchi, and piping hot coffee had been set on the table.

Kyung-A wore a sky-blue robe and a pair of embroidered slippers. Her beautiful, shoulder-length hair smelled of perfumed soap. She wore no make-up and her face showed not even a trace of wrinkles. As she bent over to pour him a cup of steaming black coffee, her mother-of-pearl breasts nearly cascaded out of her robe.

Like flowing water, he thought, vaguely aware of a strange uneasiness. His mother's legs, soft as chrysanthemum petals,

141

showed themselves through the slit in her robe. He lowered his eyelashes respectfully.

His mother was humming a tune to herself. There was a salubrious lilt to her humming, suggestive of lusty sentiments. She looked suspiciously content.

"I thought I heard a noise last night," he said, feigning nonchalance.

"Did you? What kind of noise?"

"Voices. I thought I heard someone talking. Was someone here?"

He imagined her weighing his words, calculating his intent, measuring her possible responses.

"Don't be silly," she answered, removing a pot from the stove. "You must have been dreaming."

"Sure."

This answer, so natural and plausible, was not at all what he had expected. His imagination had obviously gotten the better of him.

"Pleasant dreams?"

He shrugged. Since waking up his sluggish mind could barely muster enough energy to function, let alone recall the vagaries of his unconscious during the night. However, prompted by his mother's question, Yoo-Min's image eerily wafted up. Transfigured by death, she resembled a department store mannequin. With his heart wildly palpitating, he thought: *Was it just a dream? Or was it real?*

Yoo-Min's ice-blue image imploded without a trace.

He dimly heard his mother speaking to him, but the words were drowned out by the question thundering in his head:

Is she dead?

Huddled over his desk, Kwang-Chul buried his head in his hands and struggled to keep his composure. For the umpteenth time that morning, he asked himself whether Yoo-Min was indeed dead. Uncertainty plagued his thoughts like a tapeworm eating away at his brain.

Out of sheer habit, he opened up his dream journal despite his loathing to do so. Turning to a fresh page, he reached for his pen and with trembling hand recorded his dream of the previous night. Twice, he put down his pen in mid-sentence while he agonized over the propriety of setting down on paper his reminiscences of his dream. But consistency prevailed and after considerable effort he finally succeeded in writing down the details of his dream as he remembered them, leaving nothing out.

Gnawing at the knuckle of his thumb, Kwang-Chul struggled to remember his dream, but the sensations and images that flooded his brain were far too disturbing. He remembered only with absolute certainty Yoo-Min's body limp with death, fingertips draped over her chest, every glimmer of light gone from her almond eyes. Her petrified beauty did not stir him so much as the thought that the immensity of life that had once dwelled inside her was forever gone.

For as long as he could remember, he had never cried. But the thought that Yoo-Min might be dead brought pools of grief to his eyes. Not even the goodness of his heart and the innocence of his spirit mattered so much anymore. Life seemed to him as meaningless as a gob of spit.

Gazing through tear-filled eyes at the brightly-colored figurine of the Pongsan masked dancer on his desk, he closed the journal and clutched it to his chest.

Looking out his window, he saw the sun poking a hole through a layer of clouds, irradiating the world with goodness, purifying its imperfections. He decided that getting out for a little sunshine would do him some good.

All day he wandered aimlessly about Seoul on foot. The previous night's storm had cleared the air of the thick miasma of smog that invariably hung over the city, transforming the ugly gray haze of the sky into a vivid cerulean.

Shuffling along the pavement, he wended his way through the teeming crowds and heavy traffic, unheedful of everything but an image of Yoo-Min burning darkly in his mind, threatening to sear a hole in his head.

Before long he found himself in Myeong-dong. He made his way to the teashop where just the day before he sat and had tea with Miss Kim and chatted about King Mu, the three Maitreyas, and sundry other things. It seemed so long ago now, as if it had all happened in another lifetime.

Through the window of the teashop he saw a girl with lustrous black hair sitting alone at a table, and he wildly thought:

It's her!

Rapture unfolded its glorious wings across his heart. Real happiness, distant and unattainable for so long, was closer that it had ever been before.

The girl looked his way. Her eyes met his with a harsh iciness. He was suddenly aware of a sinking feeling in his stomach, an all-too-familiar emptiness, and at once he knew that it was too good to be true – it wasn't Yoo-Min after all.

For a few moments after that, he contemplated his brush with the impossible.

He entered the teashop and took a seat at one of the low, double-paneled, black and gold lacquered tables. There was no one in the teashop except the girl he had seen through the window. She was drinking tea and staring out the window. He was sure she was making a deliberate show of ignoring his presence. A tranquil, meditative melody playing over a pair of acoustic speakers in the corners of the mahogany ceiling drifted through the room.

Miss Kim appeared out of nowhere. She was wearing a royal blue hanbok and gold flower chandelier earrings. Her shiny black hair was pinned up in a bun with a gold and lapus lazuli flower hair pin decoration.

"I see you're back," she said, flashing a friendly smile. Her pearly-white teeth sparkled through fuchsia-painted lips. "Would you like some tea?"

"Yes, thank you."

"It'll just take a moment."

While he waited for Miss Kim to bring him tea, he idly studied the double-paneled tabletop and marveled at its magnificent artwork depicting peacocks and cranes perched on flowering branches. A green mountain rose in the background. The panels were mounted on a black-painted leg base. Though he was by no means an expert on antiques, he judged the lacquer work to be late eighteenth century; he surmised that the table would fetch a decent price at an auction house.

Miss Kim returned with a sterling silver serving tray. On it were a blue porcelain teapot, a cup and saucer, and a large book covered in an Asian brocade fabric with a pink background and gold dragons. She arranged the tea set in front of him and poured him a cup of tea.

145

"This is a very soothing tea. It will relax you and free your mind from the clutter of your thoughts."

Kwang-Chul acknowledged her with a nod, trying to hide his disappointment. He had been hoping for the same elaborate service as the day before. He leaned forward and tapped the lacquered surface of the table.

"I like this. It's very picturesque."

"Yes, isn't it? A lot of our customers like it."

"If you look at it long enough, you almost wish that you could be somewhere as peaceful and beautiful as the scene on the table. Somewhere long ago, I guess."

"It does have that effect, doesn't it?"

Steam from the teacup rose and tweaked his nostrils. He savored the mild aroma and found it to his liking. Its fragrant scent evoked in him a feeling of contentment. Sighing wistfully, he said, "The flute music, too. It's light and airy and makes one feel that one's in a different era. In fact, quite honestly, this whole teashop plays upon the senses in a most peculiar way. You get the feeling when you walk through that front door that you're walking into the past."

Gazing upon Miss Kim, he thought that she, too, seemed to come right out of the past. She looked like a Chosŏn princess in her royal blue hanbok and gold flower chandelier earrings.

"Some of our customers have said exactly the same thing," said Miss Kim, her black jade eyes glimmering through long, willowy lashes.

He breathed deeply and glanced around as if to more fully appreciate his surroundings. "Every so often I wish I could escape into the past."

"Why is that?" asked Miss Kim politely. She stood over him, staring thoughtfully at the top of his head.

"I don't know why. It's a just a feeling I have. A longing, really. Sometimes I think it's a longing for my destiny."

"History has a way of repeating itself," said Miss Kim offhandedly. She walked over to an antique paulownia wood cabinet adorned with intricately designed silver hardware. "Maybe you just feel its cyclical patterns."

Through the slits of his eyes he watched as Miss Kim picked up a crystal decanter and gazed at it soberly. The afternoon sunlight blazing through the window warmed him to the point of drowsiness. His eyes drifted to the beautiful hand-painted tableau as he relaxed to the soothing sounds of a bamboo flute that played in the background. The haunting, ethereal notes evoked in him a strong yearning for the past.

"Do you think so? I feel it's more than that. Sometimes I'm on the verge of remembering something, but I don't know what. I just wish I could remember."

Succumbing to a surfeit of pleasant sensations, he yawned prodigiously. The confluence of tea, the late afternoon sunlight streaming through the window, and the coziness of the teashop with all its peculiar charms was having a soporific effect on him. His eyes languidly fell on the lavishly embellished book resting on the silver serving tray. Reaching over, he casually picked up the ornate book and flipped through it. Faded hanja characters – the classical Chinese style of writing using the Idu system for prose – were handwritten on each warm, white tone page in India ink. Events preceding the fall of Paekche during the time of King Ŭija and Queen Ŭn'go unfolded across each page.

For a moment he thought fantastically that the book might be a copy of the *Ku samguk sa,* the fabled history upon which the *Samguk sagi* was largely based. But he immediately

147

conceded the absurdity of such a notion. The *Ku samguk sa* had long been lost, and besides, the faint characters in the book were almost certainly the handiwork of Miss Kim. As he read further, he couldn't help but smile. Miss Kim was undoubtedly a woman of wild imagination.

As the filtered sunlight toasted his face and the comforting tea warmed his belly, he slipped effortlessly into a misty reverie. Against the dappled backdrop of his mind he saw Queen Ŭn'go with tears staining her cheeks as she watched several thousand court ladies hurl themselves off a rock atop the cliff overlooking Paekma River into the swirling waters below. The court ladies looked like spring blossoms as their colorful hanboks billowed in the updraft; they seemed to gently dance in the air, like petals of flowers caught in a breeze. Only now it wasn't Queen Ŭn'go who tearfully gazed upon the ladies, it was the enigmatic Miss Kim. Had the court ladies really been pushed off Nakhwaam Cliff, as Miss Kim had intimated?

His eyelids drooped as an agreeable somnolence crept over him. Through a web of lashes he saw Miss Kim set down the decanter and sadly smile at him.

"Perhaps it's better not to remember," he heard her softly say just before he dozed off.

When he awoke, he was surprised to see that the teashop was empty. The girl who had been drinking tea by herself was gone. The mysterious book was no longer there. Miss Kim was nowhere to be found. He called out for her several times, but when she didn't answer he threw some money on the table and left.

He walked for what seemed like hours. The buildings of Seoul were slowly painted in shadows by an invisible hand. Eventually he made his way to back to Glade.

The place was hopping. His mother was nowhere in sight. Chan-Woo was behind the bar dusting off a bottle of Jinro Gold. He joined his friend at the bar and ordered soju. Chan-Woo opened the bottle and poured him a glass. He drank it straight down and slammed the glass on the brushed steel bar top and told Chan-Woo to pour him another.

"Mind telling me what's going on?" asked Chan-Woo, pouring himself a glass and guzzling it down.

Kwang-Chul glanced wearily at his friend.

"Where's Yoo-Min?"

"How should I know? Say, you don't look so good. What's going on?"

Kwang-Chul downed the second glass of soju and wiped his mouth with his sleeve.

"My dreams! Let me tell you about my dreams!"

As the soju warmed his thoughts, Chan-Woo's eyes glowed like white hot coals.

"Tell me everything!"

And Kwang-Chul did. He told his friend how he hated the world because it was wicked and debauched, and how there wasn't a person in it who wasn't corrupt in his or her heart. Next he told Chan-Woo how the ugliness in the hearts of men and women everywhere was like a patina blotting out the natural beauty of their souls. Then he told Chan-Woo about the five abstentions that could free the soul from its bondage: no killing, no stealing, no lying, no alcohol, and no sex. Then he told Chan-Woo how a man must strive to rise above the ordinary in all things, how it was a man's duty to reject the small, the insignificant, the petty, and especially to forgo the pleasures of the mundane –

only then could a man discover what was true and worthwhile. Then he told Chan-Woo how Yoo-Min had walked into Glade and how he had known in an instant that *she* was the one true reality he had been seeking all his life.

Then he hung his head and told Chan-Woo about the terrible desires that raged through him day and night, plaguing him like a pestilence. He sheepishly went on to admit to all the sordid dreams he had had and to the dream journal he kept. Finally, he confessed to his dreams about Yoo-Min.

When he finished, he shook his head sadly and said, "All my life I've struggled to get a heightened sense of what's true and real. Now I can't tell anymore what's real and what isn't."

Chan-Woo exploded with laughter. "Such nonsense! You talk about reality as if it has nothing to do with this world, as if it's some fantastic paradise that can only be found somewhere beyond this world. You hate the world because it doesn't fit into your vision of what the world should be like. You think it's an illusion, something that really doesn't exist, or if it does, something that's base and vile and beneath you. But the world is bigger than you and all of your ridiculous ideas put together." Chan-Woo pounded down his soju and poured himself another glass. "You talk about love the same way. Get real, Kwang-Chul. Love's a festering stink hole of false promises and broken hearts."

Kwang-Chul felt himself shrink into the shadows as Chan-Woo stood up and towered over him larger than ever before.

"Now you listen to me. You keep having these dreams because you're not getting any boji," said Chan-Woo heatedly. "You shun the pleasures of the flesh because you

150

think the flesh is keeping you from perceiving the truth. You stupid ass! The only reality that matters *is* the flesh! Don't you know anything about biology? Man's dominated by an incessant desire to copulate. It's our nature. There's nothing wrong with it either."

"You're wrong," protested Kwang-Chul. Shafts of multicolored light from an overhead disco ball illuminated his moon-shaped face with a variegated pattern. He held out his empty glass and Chan-Woo filled both their glasses up. "I don't care about boji."

"Liar! *Every* guy cares about boji, whether he admits it or not!" exclaimed Chan-Woo, shoving a finger in Kwang-Chul's face. "We want it at all costs and we'll do anything to get it. We'll spend money in pursuit of it; we'll sacrifice our principles, our friends, even our loved ones for it, because there's nothing that excites us more, nothing that drives us to such incredible distraction or kindles our imagination so greatly. During the day, thoughts of it continuously creep into our heads like venom in our blood; at night we can't sleep because we burn with desire for it. Everything we do, everything we say, is motivated in one way or another by our desire for boji."

Kwang-Chul flushed lobster red. The color was more pronounced from the effects of the soju. "The inferior man lusts for the flesh; the superior man yearns for the spirit," he said testily.

Chan-Woo gazed at him as if a strange bug had appeared before him. He guzzled down his glass of soju. Stoked with sudden inspiration, he said, "Look, bonehead, you wanted the truth. I'm *giving* you the truth! There's no difference between the flesh and the spirit! It's all the same! You want to find Buddha or God or whatever you believe in? You think you're going to find Him *out there*? God isn't *out there*,

Kwang-Chul! He's here, and here, and here! He's everywhere! You see this table? That's God! You see this chair? That's God! You see this bottle of soju? That's God! A girl's boji? That's God, too! Yes, *especially* a girl's boji!" Unzipping his pants, Chan-Woo pulled out his jaji and waved it around with his hand. "Here's God, too!"

Chan-Woo danced about boisterously. Several of the patrons looked over to see what all the commotion was about. With jaji in hand, Chan-Woo gleefully shouted, "Don't be alarmed! It's only God! Here he is! Take a look at God, everyone!"

Mortified by his friend's behavior, Kwang-Chul pleaded, "Put that away, please! You're going to chase our customers away!"

Chan-Woo rammed his jaji back into his pants. "The truth scares you, doesn't it? The truth is so simple, it's beautiful! It's people like you, Kwang-Chul, with all your highfalutin notions of purity and virtue who make it ugly." Pouring another glass of soju, Chan-Woo gulped it down and looked Kwang-Chul straight in the eye. "You talk about Yoo-Min as if she's something special. You think she's the one and only girl for you, the girl of your dreams. Well, let me tell you, there's nothing special about her, Kwang-Chul. There's nothing special about *any* girl. They're just girls, that's all. Don't you get it?"

Kwang-Chul swiped at the tears welling in his eyes. He had never seen the fire in Chan-Woo's eyes blaze so strongly. Chan-Woo spoke with the conviction of a man who intimately knew the truth.

"Look," Chan-Woo said, laying a hand on Kwang-Chul's shoulder. "Do yourself a favor. Forget all that metaphysical crap you waste your time on. You want enlightenment? I'll enlighten you! What's here and now is all that matters.

What you see is what you get. Now quit living in your dreams. If you love Yoo-Min so much, just tell her. What are you afraid of? If she feels the same way about you, she'll let you know. If not, go find yourself a real live girl somewhere – one you can touch and hold in your arms and make love to every night. You'll be a much happier person."

Suddenly one of the hostesses, a full-figured girl in a sexy, slit miniskirt and spike heels, appeared at their side. Nah-Young was a personal favorite of Chan-Woo. She sidled up to him and let him slip his arm around her waist.

"Isn't that right, baby?" Chan-Woo asked her, as if she had been part of the conversation all along.

"Isn't what right?" she asked, puzzled.

Chan-Woo winked at Kwang-Chul. "That I love you," he said, planting a kiss on Nah-Young's cheek.

Nah-Young's face glowed with happiness.

As if on cue, the lights in Glade grew romantically dim. As darkness closed around Kwang-Chul, a formidable doubt loomed in his mind:

Is it really that simple? Have I been wrong about everything?

That night after Glade closed Kwang-Chul looked out the window and noticed a figure soaked in darkness across the street. Fingers of ice traced themselves down his back as the nebulous shape emerged into the bright light of a street lamp and took on a distinct clarity – a young, heroic-looking figure standing about one hundred and eighty-eight centimeters tall and marvelously chiseled, something more than a man but less than a god: Suk-Jun.

And just like that, Suk-Jun was gone. The street was desolate except for a stray cat. Kwang-Chul couldn't help but wonder whether he had imagined the whole thing.

The episode was still on his mind when he went upstairs for bed. He was surprised to find that his mother was still awake. She was curled up on a pile of pillows in her favorite robe, the silk one with a female tigress embroidered on the back, with a bowl of silkworm larvae at her side. She was sobbing quietly and dabbing at her reddened eyes with a crumpled tissue.

He stopped dead in his tracks. His blood congealed as he recognized the black notebook in his mother's lap – his dream journal. He braced himself for a torrent of angry words.

"I was crying because I had a dream about your father," his mother sniffed. She dabbed at her nose with the sleeve of her robe. "I miss him so much."

He stood dumbly, caught off guard by her remark. Of all the things he thought she would say, he hadn't expected this.

"My diary," his mother said, nodding at the notebook in her lap. "I was just reading from it." He nodded as her words sunk into his head. She added wistfully, "I loved your father so much."

"Father loved you very much, too," he said softly, struck by his mother's sincerity. But then, not really knowing what else to say, he wished her good night and pleasant dreams, leaving her alone with her memories.

Seeking the solitude of his room, he sat at his desk and sighed deeply. The certainties of his youth seemed less certain now. Perhaps his mother had actually loved his father and this love had been strong enough to see through superficialities and grasp the essence of a man. And perhaps he had been wrong about his father all along. What he had taken for ordinariness were the calm, steady ways of a man who knew his course in life, whose arrow was shot straight and true to the mark.

He turned his head and gazed unseeingly at the figurine of the Pongsan masked dancer on his desk. All along he had believed that somewhere in the world was a girl who was meant just for him and that he was meant just for her. The love between them would be so powerful that it would transform his mundane life into something quite extraordinary and even spectacular.

And then *she* appeared. Yoo-Min attracted him inexplicably and irresistibly, fired his imagination such that he regarded her as something beyond the ordinary, something amazing and perhaps even miraculous. But when he couldn't have her in real life, he sought her in his dreams.

Kwang-Chul sat back and pondered his dreams. Recalling that he had once read that dreams were caused by the random firing of neurons in the brain, he decided:

Chan-Woo's right. My dreams are just dreams, nothing more.

Laughing to himself with this revelation, Kwang-Chul felt the ki stirring within him, rising up through the vertebrae of his spine like a serpent unloosening its coils. The clearness of his mind was like that of an unmarred jewel. He had seldom experienced moments of such utter clarity in his life.

He knew what he must do. He no longer yearned for escape from the world; instead, he longed to find his happiness in the world. His heart now clamored for the simple, ordinary things in life that he had previously disdained. From this moment on, he told himself, he would no longer aspire to be different from others. He would be content to be just like everyone else.

Seeing the journal on his desk, he reached over for it and held it doubtfully in his hands. Its pages no longer held any meaning for him. With a grunt, he tossed it into the wastebasket by the side of his desk. Tomorrow he would burn its pages.

Stripping off his clothes and tumbling into bed, he crawled between the sheets and felt their smooth, palpable texture with his fingertips. His bed was solid and real and deliciously comfortable.

Closing his eyes, he watched as Yoo-Min's face gently floated in and out of his mind like a silvery flower swept downstream by the currents of a flowing river. He vaguely thought:

Tomorrow will be different. When I see Yoo-Min, I'll let her know how I feel about her. I have a feeling that everything will be alright . . .

That night he dreamt he was standing on a path leading up the side of a great hill. Mount Ong. The sky above him was flawlessly blue. He felt completely at peace with himself.

The touch of a hand on his shoulder. When he whirled around, a girl with a mark of great beauty stood before him. Jung-Sin. She said to him, "It's you. You found me. I knew that one day you would."

"Yes, it's me."

"I didn't recognize you. It's been so long."

"More than a thousand years."

He drew her into his arms. It felt to him as if she belonged there, had always belonged there. The emptiness that permeated his existence was no longer there.

He gazed rapturously into her eyes. Her dark almond eyes were bottomless pools that drew him into them. He sunk deeper and deeper into the vortex of her soul. He closed his eyes and whirled dizzily in a sea of madness.

When he opened his eyes again, she was gone.

The furnishings in his room wheeled recklessly about, then planted themselves squarely in place.

A flash of gold caught his eye. Suk-Jun was standing over him. How was it possible? Suk-Jun must be one who had attained the six supernatural powers, the fifth of which was the power to be anywhere at will.

The darkness in Suk-Jun's eyes spelled trouble. He smoothed his hand over his head and felt his mole in the shape of the yang taiji. Comprehension flooded his mind. Yoo-Min and Jung-Sin. Kwang-Chul and Suk-Jun. Kwallŭk and Han-Yong. The ripples of time spreading out in ever-widening circles. The circle was complete. Jung-Sin and Yoo-Min. Han-Yong and Kwallŭk. Clouds of confusion rolled across his mind. Which one was he?

A blur of red, white, and yellow came into focus. Suk-Jun was holding the figurine of the Pongsan masked dancer above his head. Kwang-Chul didn't know whether he was dreaming or awake. It seemed so real.

As dawn's light poured through the window, the figurine came crashing down on his face.

NOTES

Chapter One

Yo. A traditional Korean mattress.

Ibul. A traditional Korean quilt.

Ondol. A Korean heating system in which the floor is heated.

Samguk sagi. *History of the Three Kingdoms,* compiled by historian Kim Pusik in the 12th century. The *Samguk sagi* is a historical record of the three kingdoms of Korea – Koguryo, Silla, and Paekche – which existed from 57 B.C. until 668 A.D., when Silla conquered Koguryo and unified the Korean peninsula.

Samguk yusa. *Memorabilia of the Three Kingdoms,* compiled by Iryŏn in the 13th century. The *Samguk yusa* is a collection of legends, tales, and folklore relating to the three kingdoms of Korea.

King Hŏngang. (875-886). The forty-ninth king of Silla.

Ch'ŏyong. The story of Ch'ŏyŏng is found in the Samguk yusa. King Hŏngang of Silla rewarded his faithful servant with a beautiful wife. Each night while Ch'ŏyŏng was away from home, a demon spirit, attracted by her beauty, descended in human form and made love to her. One night Ch'ŏyong returned home after a night of celebration to see four legs in bed. Two legs belonged to his wife, but whose were the other two?

Chapter Two

Yin taiji. The yin taiji refers to the yin half of the taiji or yin-yang symbol, symbolizing the female (moon).

Kangsu. (d. 692). Renowned Confucian scholar during the reign of King Muyŏl of Silla.

Paekche. One of the Three Kingdoms of ancient Korea. According to the *Samguk sagi*, Paekche was founded in 18 B.C. by Onjo, the son of Chumong, founder of Koguryŏ. The kingdom continued in existence until 660 A.D., when it was destroyed by the combined forces of Silla and T'ang China. Thirty-one kings ruled Paekche from 18 B.C. to 660 A.D.

Hyech'ong. A Paekche monk. The *Nihon Shoki* (or *Nihongi*), an ancient Japanese historical text, places the arrival of Hyech'ong at the Japanese court in 595.

Vinaya rules of discipline. Monastic rules of discipline in Buddhism.

King Sŏng. The twenty-sixth king of Paekche, who reigned from 523-554.

Sanskrit texts of Wu-fen lü. The Mahīsāsaka five-part Vinaya.

Where royal decree had even ordered . . . During the reign of King Pŏp (r. 599-600).

T'ang China to trample this wonderful flower . . . In 660. Silla and T'ang China combined forces to conquer Paekche. In 668, Silla and T'ang China combined forces once again to conquer neighboring Koguryŏ, thereby unifying the Three Kingdoms.

Silla blood flowed through his veins . . . Kwang-Chul's surname is Kim, which is the name of one of clans that ruled ancient Silla.

It'aewon-dong. A district of Seoul popular with tourists for its restaurants and drinking houses.

Soju. A rice-based distilled liquor originating during the 13th century.

Anju. Bar food, such as dried squid, fish, peanuts.

Coiled serpent. A reference to *kundalini*, a psychic energy described in Hindu teachings as laying dormant at the base of the spine like a coiled serpent.

Kayageum. A twelve-string zither originating in ancient Kaya. The kingdom of Kaya was contemporaneous with the Three Kingdoms and might be considered the fourth kingdom of ancient Korea.

Chapter Three

Pongsan masked dance. A masked dance play originating in the Pongsan region in Hwanghae province. The dance is accompanied by music, songs, satirical speech, gags and gestures, and ends with the dancers burning their masks to repel evil spirits.

Mugunghwa. Korea's national flower. Known in the west as "rose of Sharon" *(Hibiscus syriacus).*

Seodaemun-gu. A district of Seoul.

Wŏn-Hyo. (617-686). A renown Silla monk.

Palsim suhaeng chang. *(Arouse Your Mind and Practice!)* A work of Wŏn-Hyo exhorting the practice of meditation.

Saint Ignatius Loyola. (1491-1556).

Manual for spiritual exercises. The autograph "Spiritual Exercises." The actual autograph has been lost. A quarto copy with corrections in the author's handwriting remains, as does a Latin translation probably made by St. Ignatius, dated 1541.

Chapter Four

Yeouido. An island on the edge of the Han River; the business and banking center of Seoul.

Ch'ojok. Korean flute made from blades of grass.

White veil. In Korea, the color white is associated with death.

Chapter Five

Chaebol. A conglomerate of Korean companies usually controlled by one family.

Angmanun Prada-rul Ipnunda. *The Devil Wears Prada*, by Lauren Weisberger.

Cyworld. A popular social network site like Facebook or MySpace.

Minihompy. Mini home page

Chungcheongnam-do. A province in the west of South Korea.

Light as leaves and closer than air. Echoing a line from Ezra Pound's poem, *Speech for Psyche in the Golden Book of Apuleius*. Each night the god Cupid, concealed by the darkness, lay with the mortal Psyche, who marveled at the weight of him.

Chapter Six

Bori-cha. Roasted barley tea.

Kimchi. Fermented vegetables, such as cabbage or radishes, seasoned with hot pepper and spices.

Hyangga. Korean songs written in hyangch'al, or Chinese characters, composed from the seventh to the tenth centuries. Twenty-five have survived to the present time.

Hangul. Korean alphabet developed during the reign of King Sejŏng of Chosŏn (r. 1418-50). The Chosŏn dynasty lasted from 1392 to 1910 and is believed to be the longest reigning dynasty in East Asia.

Hyangch'al. The Korean language written in Chinese characters.

Queen Chinsŏng. (r. 887-897). Queen Chinsŏng ruled during the decline of Unified Silla and during the period of the Later Three Kingdoms, which lasted from 892-936.

Taegu. A Silla monk commissioned by Queen Chinsŏng to compiles a collection of hyangga. In 888 monk Taegu and Wihong, a Silla minister, completed the compilation, called *Samdaemok (Collection of Hyangga from the Three Periods of Silla History).*

Boshintang. Dog meat soup. Eating dog meat is a long-standing tradition in Korean culture. Although the sale and consumption of dog meat is illegal in Korea, the practice continues.

Dog days of summer. The three dog days of summer *(sambok)* in the Korean lunar calendar are July 18 *(cholbok)*, July 27 *(chungbok)*, and August 17 *(malbok)*. These are recognized as the hottest days of the year. Dog meat is eaten in the belief that it replenishes the body's energy during these sweltering summer days. It is also believed that eating dog meat will enhance virility.

Kisaeng. Courtesans trained to entertain men with song, poetry, and witty conversation.

Jindo. A Korean hunting dog originally from Jindo Island in South Korea.

Yellow dog. Nureongi, a type of dog bred primarily for meat, considered the best dog for eating in Korea.

Bibimpap. A popular Korean dish of white rice, vegetables, meat, egg, and chili pepper.

Soon dubu. Spicy tofu stew or soup.

Makkoli. A type of milky-white rice wine.

Dongdongju. Rice wine similar to *makkoli* but with grains of rice floating on the surface.

Galbi. Beef or pork ribs, usually grilled.

Chapter Seven

Four-Seven Debate. A famous philosophical debate during the Chosǒn dynasty over the roles of *i* (principle) and *ki* (material force) that took place in an exchange of letters between Yi Hwang and Ki Taesŭng. The debate was continued by Yi I with his friend Sŏng Hon.

Chapter Nine

Myeong-dong. One of the main shopping areas of Seoul.

Hanbok. Traditional Korean dress.

Chapter Ten

Mount Ong. Located in Ungju (now South Chungcheong Province) in ancient Paekche. Mount Ong is associated with the Silla monk Hyŏngwang, who was a native of Ungju. Hyŏngwang traveled to China where he learned the Lotus Scripture and reputedly attained the Lotus Samādhi. Upon his return to Ungju, he built a small hermitage on Mount Ong in Paekche. One day he disappeared as was never heard from again.

Kwallŭk. The monk Kwallŭk appears in the *Nihon Shoki.* In 602, he was sent to Japan by Paekche to spread the teachings of Buddhism. The date of his birth and death are unknown.

Eight liberations. The eight liberations are: perception of form while remaining in the fine material sphere; perception of external form but not one's own form; confidence attained through the appreciation of beauty; overcoming the perceptions of form and abiding in boundless space; overcoming the sphere of boundless space and abiding in the plane of unbounded consciousness; overcoming the plane of unbounded consciousness and abiding in the sphere of nothingness; overcoming the sphere of nothingness and abiding in the sphere of neither perception nor non-perception; overcoming the sphere of neither perception nor non-perception and reaching the extinction of perception and sensation.

Ten wholesome deeds. Abstaining from killing, stealing, sexual unrestraint and misconduct, lying, harsh and malicious speech, divisive speech, gossiping, covetousness, anger and hatred, and foolishness.

Four noble truths. All life is suffering; all suffering is caused by desire; the cessation of suffering is attained through the eradication of desire; and there is a path to the cessation of suffering which leads to the end of the cycle of rebirth.

Twelvefold chain of dependent origination. Ignorance, action, consciousness, mind and form, sensory perception, contact, feeling, desire, attachment, existence, birth, and decay and death.

Six perfections. The perfection of generosity, morality, patience, effort, meditation, and wisdom.

Bodhisattva. An enlightened being or one on the path to enlightenment.

Otgoreum. An ornamental ribbon that is tied into a bow and hung vertically down the front of the hanbok.

Chapter Eleven

Ssirum. Korean wrestling. Ssirum is the national sport of Korea.

Paektu class. The heavyweight class; one of four weight classes in Korean wrestling which are named after four famous mountain peaks in Korea.

Sapta. A sash belt worn around the waist and thigh.

Ddeok. Korean rice cake.

Japchae. Korean dish made with cellophane noodles, vegetables, and sesame oil.

Pogolchi. Bu Gu Zhi (Chinese) or *Psoralea*. Chinese herb used to restore vitality and for treating diarrhea.

Taeksa. Ze Xie (Chinese), also known as *Alisma orientalis Alismataceae* or simply *Alisma*. Used for treating diarrhea.

Maitreya. A future incarnation of Buddha.

King Mu. 600–641.

Pangjang. The Korean name for Fang-Chang, a mythical island in Chinese legend where souls who have attained immortality dwell.

King Mu had a lake dug . . . In 634.

Anapchi. An artificial pond constructed during the reign of King Munmu of Silla (661-681), famous for its beauty.

Kyŏngju. Capital of the ancient kingdom of Silla.

Mireuksa temple. The largest Buddhist temple in ancient Paekche, built by King Mu in 602.

General Kyebaek. Paekche military leader who led his troops against the invading Silla force in 660. Before departing for battle, he reportedly killed his wife and children to prevent them from being captured and enslaved.

Kim Yusin. (595-673).

Battle of Hwangsanbul. In 660.

Chapter Twelve

Koku. Around April 20.

Ipha. The fifth or sixth of May.

Sŏn. Zen.

Sravaka. A disciple of Buddha.

Pratyekabuddha. One who has attained enlightenment without a teacher.

Three knowledges. Knowledge of past lives, knowledge of the laws of karma, and knowledge of extinction of the outflows.

Kihwa. (1376-1433). A Buddhist monk during the late Koryo and early Chosŏn period.

Chapter Thirteen

Six supernatural powers. Telepathy, clairvoyance, clairaudience, the power to remember past lives, the power to be anywhere or do anything at will, and knowledge how to extinguish the outflows.

Ch'eng Hao. (1032-1085). A Chinese philosopher.

Sŏ Kyŏngdŏk. (1489-1546). A neo-Confucianist from the Chosŏn dynasty.

Chapter Fifteen

Gangnam Style. A hit song by the South Korean musician PSY.

Pyongyang cigarettes. North Korean cigarettes sold cheaply in the street markets of Seoul.

Chapter Sixteen

Taekbaek mountains. A mountain range stretching across North and South Korea.

Chapter Seventeen

Facing a wall. Refers to a Zen sitting meditation. Legend has it that Bodhidharma sat facing a wall in meditation at Shaolin temple for nine years.

Biblical admonition. "And if thy right eye offend thee, pluck it out, and cast it from thee: for it is profitable for thee that one of thy members should perish, and not that thy whole body should be cast into hell." Matt. 5:29.

Hyujŏng. (1520-1602). A renown Buddhist monk of the Chosŏn dynasty.

Pou. (1515-1565). A Buddhist master during the early Chosŏn dynasty.

Il Chŏng. (*Oneness and Correctness*). A treatise seeking to reconcile the differences between Confucianism and Buddhism.

Ki (or *chi). In Eastern philosophies, the vital force of the universe that creates and maintains life.

Buk sori. A Korean peasant drum song.

Chapter Eighteen

Cheonjiyeon. A famous waterfall on Cheju Island off the coast of South Korea.

Changgo. The *changgo* or *seyogo* is an hourglass-shaped drum with two heads which, when played simultaneously, represent the harmony between man and woman.

Hanwha. A Korean manufacturer of fireworks.

Hangang Park. A park in Yeouido, Seoul and scene of the annual Seoul International Fireworks Festival.

Chapter Nineteen

King Ŭija. (r. 641-660). The thirty-first and last king of Paekche.

Ku samguk sa. (*Old History of the Three Kingdoms*). Cited as the most important source for the *Samguk sagi*.

Five abstentions. Also known as the five precepts.

The inferior man lusts for the flesh . . . *Cf.* Confucius, *Analects*, 4:16. ("The superior man seeks what is right, the inferior man seeks what is profitable.")

Yang taiji. The yang taiji refers to the yang half of the taiji or yin-yang symbol, symbolizing the male (sun).